MAGNOLIA & DIOR 2

A Hood Love Story

MISS JAZZIE

Magnolia & Dior 2

Copyright © 2022 by Miss Jazzie

All rights reserved.

Published in the United States of America.

Published by Cole Hart Signature, LLC.

Mailing List

To stay up to date on new releases, plus get information on contests, sneak peeks, and more,

Go To The Website Below...

www.colehartsignature.com

I dedicate this book to my readers. I'm tired y'all, but that won't stop me from coming through for y'all. I pen every book with thoughts of my readers in mind. I'm figuring y'all out slowly but surely. What y'all like and don't like, but I know y'all love Magnolia. Thank you for allowing me to let y'all inside of my wicked mind. This is only the beginning, I promise.

MAGNOLIA

I know I've done some fucked up shit in my life. Some shit I told y'all and shit I kept to myself. Zenobia don't even know the shit I've done. If she did, our story wouldn't have gotten this far. I had to know that karma would come back to pull my ass hairs, but I didn't think it would be this soon. My mind was telling me not to trust this bitch, but her aura was what drew me in. Reeled me in like a fish on a fucking hook, and I fell for the dumb shit.

I didn't know this bitch from a can of paint. All I wanted was my medication, but she had to take it a bit further. A nigga was vulnerable as hell. In the midst of Chunky killing my daughter and me hating her, I went to the first bitch that gave me a little attention, Dior. How the fuck was I supposed to know her husband was Fhendi? She said she had a fucking husband but failed to mention the nigga's name. That nigga was fucking my wife anyway and I didn't like it. I didn't take threats lightly, so he had to fucking go. I fucked with Fhendi at one point, then the nigga just slid off the grid and popped back out years later. I didn't even know the nigga was married.

When the US Marshals dragged me out of Dior's house, I knew she'd set me up. She told me that nobody knew where the fuck she laid her head. I trusted her words, but her actions displayed something totally different. She played me, and I planned to get to the bottom of this shit when the dust settled. I knew I spat some hurtful shit at her, but I meant it. I felt in the pit of my stomach that Zenobia was in cahoots with this bitch, or maybe I wasn't thinking right. I knew my wife, or at least I thought I did. She had something to do with it. I couldn't put nothing past her conniving and deceitful ass, but I couldn't figure out the connection between them. Once I was out this shit, I would hit the pavement and wouldn't stop until I got answers.

I sat in that cold, hard ass chair that had my ass hurting for the past five hours. Them bitches tried to make me put on a striped jumper, but I refused because I wasn't a fucking criminal. They gave me pants and a white T shirt. They still managed to give me those hard orange ass slippers.

"Mahsyn Calvary, do you understand that you are being charged with capital murder of Fhendi Maverick?"

One of the detectives came in the room slamming the door and throwing a folder on the desk. I wanted to laugh because this nigga was a joke. Ain't shit he could do or say to me to intimidate me, handcuffed and all.

"I didn't kill anybody," I said calmly, because I wasn't about to give them the reaction they were looking for.

"Shouldn't you request a lawyer at this point?"

They were trying the good cop-bad cop shit, but it wasn't working. I kept my poker face on full display. Nothing they could say was gon' rock me.

"For something y'all accusing me of? Some shit I know I didn't do? Who the fuck is Fhendi? If the fuck I did kill this nigga, shouldn't y'all be drawing up the fucking paperwork to have me extradited to New Orleans?," I told them and realized I fucked up.

"Who said he was killed in New Orleans?" The smirk on the

detective's face didn't go unnoticed. I had to think quick and not act on pure emotion.

My mind was really fucked up. I was still fucked up behind my daughter, battling my feelings for Zenobia, then this bitch Dior pulling a hoe. She had to fucking know Zenobia was my wife. I was off my square fucking with Dior. Trusted the bitch too soon. She mind fucked me almost comatose because that's what she did for a living. She had people out here baring their souls and shit, and she pulled fast one on me. Went to her office for a refill on my medicine and ended up in fucking jail.

"Mr. Calvary, do you realize what is going on?" Detective Marshall Mays asked me, bringing me out my thoughts. I looked at him with a stone face.

"The feds stated that you confessed at the time of arrest." He got in my face like he was about to hit me. He was sparing his own life because I was in handcuffs. If I wasn't, I would really have a fucking murder charge on my back.

"I didn't confess to shit," I told him, my eyes turned to slits. I knew what the fuck I said, and it wasn't a confession.

"We've been watching you for some time now. You and the Masons have been on our radar for a while now," he said, and I smiled. Half the fucking Masons were cops, politicians, and FBI agents. "Our CI gave us enough information on your crew to throw the book at your back," Mays said, and I laughed harder. A fucking CI watching me from Atlanta, no fucking way.

"A CI? For what? I'm a law-abiding citizen and pay my fucking taxes just like y'all motherfuckers." I laughed, and that made their bitch asses furious. The other detective tried to yank me out the chair by the rim of my shirt, but Mays stopped him. If I left this bitch with so much as a fucking hair missing out my beard, I would own the entire state of Georgia.

"I must admit, you cleaned your record very well," Mays said.

"It was never fucking dirty," I barked at him, and he smiled. I watched as he opened the folder that he'd slammed on the desk before they tried to play that cop shit again.

He opened the folder and spread the pictures out on the table in front of me. There were pictures of me, Zenobia, Mahyesha and Ghiani, Jahari and Amerika, the entire KOE and all their wives. I really had a fucking snitch in my camp. I wasn't saying shit until I got the fuck out of here.

"How the fuck did you get those pictures?" I knew whoever it was had to be on some stalker shit. There were pictures taken from the inside of my fucking house. They even had pictures of Zenobia getting in Fhendi's fucking car. I was 38 hot. To see Chunky fucking with that nigga heavy did some shit I couldn't describe to the blood in my veins. I mean, I knew she fucked the nigga, but to even see the affection on display fucked with me. He had his arm around her waist, whispering something in her ear that had her blushing. These cracker motherfuckers were trying me, but I wouldn't give them the reaction they craved from me.

"Oh, I'm sure you know that we have our ways," Cracker Number One, who didn't have on a nametag, said. If I wasn't in handcuffs, I would have bust him in his mouth.

He kept pulling pictures from the folder. This cracker had the nerve to pull out a picture of my baby girl, Mhyia, as she lay peacefully in her pink steel casket. That was the ultimate no-no. That was like my heart being ripped out my chest all over again. Reliving the same nightmare over and over again. I pulled and yanked at the handcuffs until I felt the blood leaking from my wrists. Even that didn't stop me. I wanted their heads on a silver fucking platter, and I wouldn't stop until they were in front of me. I could feel shit. Those motherfuckers dug deep, and I ain't like it. They knew that picture would get an reaction out of me if nothing else would. Not even the pictures of Fhendi and Zenobia rocked me like my baby girl did. They went a little further and pulled a picture of Fhendi's decapitated body. I wanted to chuckle because they really thought they were going to get a confession out of me, but they weren't. They were really trying to pull every trick out the hat.

"The fuck is that?" I asked, perplexed. I had zoned out because I couldn't think of one person who would do me dirty. It had to be someone close to me. This wasn't how I moved. I was clean. Everything I did was with precision and expertise. The only person who knew what I'd done was Zenobia, and her loyalty to me overpowered her entire existence. I didn't give a fuck what we were going through, she would never be a snake ass bitch. I stood ten toes on that.

"I'm sure you know exactly who that is," Cracker said, banging his fist on the picture, breaking me from my thoughts.

I think he was madder than me because he couldn't get me to confess to some shit I didn't do. I had no clue who this dead nigga was on the pictures, and that was facts. That was not Fhendi's body parts on those pictures because I made Zenobia burn Fhendi's ass to teach her a lesson. I took care of Nhacarri's body myself because she was my problem and I'd brought her into our lives. They were ashes to ashes and dust to fucking dust, so I knew these pictures were straight bullshit.

"Are you done?" I asked him calmly. I guess my adrenaline had gone down, because my wrists were burning like hell.

"We just getting started, motherfucker," Cracker said. This nigga must've had a personal vendetta against me or some shit, but I didn't even know him. The venom in his eyes spoke volumes. Every time Mays tried to talk, Cracker cut his words, saying stupid shit like he knew me personally.

"Ease up on the profanity, big fella, it's not a good look for you," I told him, laughing because every tactic he tried wouldn't work with me, and he was furious. It was an epic fail. Cracker tried to lunge at me, but Mays pulled him back just in time.

"Be easy, Jason," Mays told him, and I put his name in my mental rolodex to look into later.

"You ready for your lawyer yet?" Mays asked me, and I smiled.

"No, but I would like my phone call that is owed to me," I told Mays but looked at Jason.

"We don't owe you shit!" Jason said, becoming enraged again.

"You might wanna get him the fuck out of here before I catch assault charges. These handcuffs gon' only hold my wrists for so long before I break them bitches and beat the fuck out of Jason."

"You don't get a fucking phone call until we get the answers we need," Jason rebutted, and I smirked.

"How can I give you answers to some shit that I don't know nothing about? Either let me go or give me my fucking phone call. Y'all need to release me because y'all ain't got nothing on me. We've been here for what, eight hours, and I'm tired as fuck. Y'all didn't book me yet so I know y'all ain't got shit. That's why I ain't calling my lawyer. Those pictures don't prove shit but I have a beautiful family and I fucked up by fucking with Dior, so y'all got a shitty ass CI," I told both of them.

"You are going to be booked for the murder of Fhendi Maverick." He paused and gave a hard look. "You were fucking his wife, you are one grimy motherfucker." Mays lifted me to my feet and brought me downstairs for booking.

We stepped on the elevator with Mays and Jason on each side of me. I was handcuffed in the front of my body. My mind was thinking of every scenario to kill these bitches, but I couldn't chance it because they would really throw the book at me for killing two agents. Jason leaned into my ear close enough that Marshall couldn't see.

"Nigger, I will bury you for killing my daughter's husband, because I know you did it. I just don't have enough evidence. You are going to need a team of lawyers fucking with me, because if the justice system don't do it, I will." I chuckled at his words because he had no idea who he was fucking with.

🌿 2 🌾

JADORE DIOR

My life was a fucking mess since the feds dragged Mahsyn out of my house. I was a fucking psychiatrist and couldn't even fix myself. I hadn't left the house since that night, and that was five nights ago. I closed down my practice, making sure all my doctors were well compensated for the leave of absence. I just couldn't focus. I couldn't call my parents because I didn't feel like hearing their I told you so's. I hadn't talked to Jhewelz and at this point, I didn't want to talk to anybody. She'd been calling and texting non-stop, but the only call I wanted was from Mahsyn, and he hadn't called yet. I needed answers from him about my husband. I'd poured my soul out to him, brought him to where I rested my head, for him to turn and do some shit like this.

I brought all this shit on myself, though. Two mountains may never meet but two people will. I prayed and prayed that God would show me a sign that Fhendi was alive, good or bad, and for the strength to handle it, and I ended up fucking his killer, but what was the reason behind it? What the fuck was Fhendi into that would get him killed? Only Mahsyn could answer those questions, and I was going to find out. I ended up falling in love with Mahsyn. It wasn't planned, but we shared similar stories.

He kept saying that me and his wife were working to set him up, but I didn't even know his fucking wife. He lashed out at me and that's when I realized that hurt people hurt people, and this shit between us shouldn't have ever happened. I looked at my ringing iPhone and noticed it was my daddy calling.

"Yeah, Daddy," I answered, because I knew he would have a mouthful to say.

"You know this motherfucker refuses to confess to killing your husband, and I showed him the pictures," was his answer. Not a how are you doing or nothing, straight to the point, no chasers.

"How do you know it's Fhendi's body, Daddy?" I asked him, because he didn't know for sure if that was him. My father had been adamant on bringing down the Masons for years but never could get enough evidence to hold them. Now he was going after the younger generation. Every time I would ask what his problem with them was, he would always tell me to stay in my place.

"Listen to what I'm saying to you. You were fucking the nigga that killed your husband, or have you forgotten?" he spat in the phone, and I wanted to hang up, but didn't out of respect for my father, but I was sick of his shit. I was tired of him trying to place the blame for Fhendi's death on the Masons. I didn't even know the group existed until he brought it up. I didn't understand why he was so fixated on solving something for a man he hated so much.

My father hated Fhendi. He always thought that Fhendi lived a secret life I knew nothing about. That may have been true, but I didn't care because he was who I loved and wanted to spend the rest of my life with. Maybe bringing down a group of gangstas overpowered the hatred he had for my husband.

"Let's be clear, Father," I told him, with my hand resting on my hip as if he could see me, "who said that Fhendi was dead?

You assuming shit is making my mind wonder if you know some shit I don't." I couldn't stop the tears as they fell down my eyes. I kept my sobs to myself because I didn't want my father to hear the weakness in my voice.

"You can't believe after all these years that he is just going to come waltzing inside your home and continue to live life with you? You need to stop believing whatever shit is in your mind and step into the real world, because he ain't coming back," he said with conviction as I flopped down on the bed. I couldn't control my anger. Hands trembling, mouth dry, mind racing, thoughts of the unthinkable were coming to the surface. I couldn't believe it, wouldn't believe it until I saw a fucking body. Not even the agents coming in here to get Mahsyn made me believe that Fhendi was dead. My father was a deceiver and a master of mind manipulation. If shit didn't go his way, he would make it go his way. It didn't matter how many bridges he had to cross or burn or people would become casualties because of his fuck ups.

"Yes, I do believe that my husband will come home to me and until then, stay the fuck out my life and let Mahsyn go, because you don't have anything to hold him!" I barked in the phone, then he cut my words.

"We can't hold him, but he will be in New Orleans Parish Prison come tomorrow," he said and disconnected the call. I threw my phone on the bed and cried until I didn't have any more tears left.

I didn't have the energy to call my mother or even Jhewelz, because I was more embarrassed than anything. To have to explain that I fucked one of my clients then go into detail about how we had gotten to this point would be suicide. My mother was so fucking passive that she would agree with just about anything I said because that was in her nature. My mother, Corrine, was a homemaker. Never had a job, all she had was a high school education. My father hindered her from doing what she loved, and that was becoming a medical doctor. Jason told her that her only position was to have his babies and take care of home while he worked and brought home the money.

I hated that she was so submissive. I remember days when my mother would spend her entire day preparing dinner fit for a king. Five-course dinner, including dessert. She and I would set the table and wait for my dad to come home. Beautiful table-cloth, only the best China set with the food to match. Dad would come home after the food had gotten cold with a box of fucking pizza and wings and put it on the table. Instead of my mother correcting him, we would clear the table and we would eat the pizza and wings. She never stood up for herself and I hated her for that. She catered to his every need and he fucked over her every chance he had. Not so much as cheating, but shit like having my mother cooking and slaving over the stove after making sure the house was clean, ironing his uniform for the week, for him to come home late and with different food. That wasn't submissive, that was stupid. I vowed to never end up like her, dumb and miserable.

My upbringing wasn't bad. I had the best of everything and did everything by the books, except become an FBI agent like my father. He begged and pleaded with me to join the force, but I declined because I wanted to become who I wanted to be not what he was, a crooked cop. When I chose to go to college to become a psychiatrist, my father cut me off. I had to find my way through school. I lived on campus at Spelman, and what my scholarships didn't pay for, financial aid did. I still graduated on time and became successful.

Thanks to Fhendi, I was debt free because that was the first thing he did when we got married, pay off all my student loans. My parents hated him because they thought he was a house full of secrets, but I looked past all of that because he treated me like a queen, and he was my king. Of course, I knew he was in the drug game, but I didn't know how deep. I didn't care to know, long as he came home to me every night. The only thing he didn't prepare me for was if he never came back. I sniffed back my tears because I knew if he was here, he would tell me tears were for the weak. I grabbed my phone about to dial Jhewelz's number because I needed her now more than ever, but my phone vibrated and my mother's pictured flashed on my screen. I was hesitant to answer it, but I did anyway because if not, she would keep calling until I picked up.

"Yes ma'am," I answered, and I could hear the smile in her voice. She was always happy to talk to me, and I was the complete opposite. I was taught to never hold a grudge, but her not standing up for me when my father cut me off was one I would hold forever. She never stood up for me when I needed her to, but I would spend hours on the phone when I was away at school with her crying because of my father's long work hours and didn't complain. I would stay on the phone and study while she cried her heart out like we were best friends. I didn't complain because I was her only child.

"Hi, beautiful, what are you up to?" It was one in the morning and here she was asking me what the fuck I was up to. She was a wonderful actress. I would even say she could be nominated for a daytime fucking Emmy, but I chose to keep my mouth closed.

"Ma, what are you really calling me for? Is Jason not home yet?" I asked, referring to my father, because that was the only time she called me in the middle of the night.

"No, he is not home, but I did have a nice talk with him and I must say that I am disappointed in you," she said, and I had to take the phone away from my ear and look at it. I put the phone back to my ear to listen.

"How could you not agree with your father? Why would you engage with the man that killed your husband, Jadore? That's unethical," she fussed at me like I was a fucking child. I didn't want to be disrespectful, but she was asking for it and I was about to let her ass have it.

"What's unethical is not standing up for me when your husband cut me off for not following in his footsteps. You so fucking submissive that you let him hinder your growth, and for what? To be Molly the Maid your whole life? What's unethical is you crying to your only fucking daughter, who just so happens to be your only friend, about her own father not coming home. You never had a backbone, Corrine, so I don't expect you to have one now, so you calling me to try and talk sense into me? I hope not, because you are barking up the wrong tree. Did he even tell you that that's not even Fhendi's body? No, because you so busy trying to get his stamp of approval that you don't give a fuck about who you trample over to get it. If I thought they had his body and the man that's arrested did it, don't you think I would be down there now to identify his body? Jason may mind fuck you, but I stopped listening to Jason a long time ago," I told her and hung up my phone, because whatever she was about to say would be some dumb shit that I didn't want to hear. It killed my soul that my mother didn't step up for me back then and clearly, she didn't have the lady balls to do it now. I wiped my tears away and dialed the number to my best friend, who would understand.

"What's up, babes, D'ussé or tequila?" she asked in a sleepy tone.

"Both," I told her as the tears rolled down my eyes.

"I'm on my way," she told me, and I hung up the phone and waited on her arrival.

❧ 3 ❧

ZENOBIA

"**W**hew, chile, that was like a breath of fresh air. That was a lot of shit to get out, but I'm glad I could talk to someone about it that would attempt to understand," I told my professor as we sat in his office after hours.

I'd linked up with him when he saw me sleeping in his class well after it was over. After I left Atlanta, courtesy of my husband, Khency helped me get settled into a nice condo close to school, which I was grateful for. I still had cash that Mahsyn told me to only touch for emergencies, and he still hadn't taken my name off any of his accounts, so he still loved me a little bit. I still had unlimited access to my two black cards as well. Khency helped me find a place, but I paid for everything. I made her keep everything on the low until I figured out my next move.

"But you as well as your husband have to understand that what you did was not done on purpose or with the intent to harm your daughter or hurt your husband, but more of a psychotic episode of post-partum. There are many ways it can be dealt with. Your situation was the first I've heard in years," Professor Donovan said and continued, "No one is to blame for what happened, not even you, because it's more of having the mental capacity to realize what you've done and how to deal with the actions behind it, and you sitting here talking to me tells me that you are sorry and are seeking redemption, but the only man to give you that is God. Seek God and your husband will follow. Let God guide your steps and don't beat yourself up about it, because there is a reason for every season and also a lesson to be learned, if not for you then in due time, God will show you." He chuckled. "And that's not something college taught me, life did. Now go ahead and enjoy your life. God has forgiven you and in time, so will your husband." His scrawny hand patted my shoulder, and he lifted his old body out the seat with my assistance.

Professor Donovan had become my person for the past few months. We would have sessions three times a week to talk about what happened with my daughter. The first few sessions, I cried the entire time. It wasn't until recently that I finally opened up and told him what happened. He didn't judge me for what I'd done but listened with the intention of helping me forgive myself and ask God for forgiveness. Mahsyn may have thought that I didn't grieve the loss of our daughter, but I did. I can't explain the feeling I felt when I put the pillow over her face. I was outside my body. I explained every feeling and thought with Donovan and he explained to me the cause and effects of experiencing post-partum.

I still didn't feel like what I did was justifiable, but he told me that that's where I had to learn to forgive myself because if not, I wouldn't be able to live the rest of my life and be a good mother to my kids that were on this side of the earth. I agreed with him, but I missed my husband. Everything about him, his scent, his touch, his protection, his craziness, I missed all that shit, but I wasn't about to fight for a marriage and be the only player in the game. I smiled at Donovan as I helped him out his seat, and we walked to the door. I didn't realize it was that late until we stepped out the building and it was dark. After parting ways with my professor, I got my keys and phone out my purse to call Amerika.

"What's up, bitch, you back in Atlanta with Magnolia crazy ass?" she asked, happy as hell, and I smiled. My girl deserved her happiness.

"No, bitch, if Mahsyn see me, he might kill me." We both laughed, but we knew it was up for me.

"Girl, Magnolia love you. I know shit is fucked up, but just know I don't blame you. He just gotta fully understand the shit and he'll come around. Yo' ass should have come up here instead of going back to New Orleans. I miss you," she whined in the phone like we were teenagers. I did miss my friend, but this was some shit I had to do on my own.

"I miss you too, but I need to do this for me," I told her.

"Bitch, you better get yo' mind right before the next bitch snatch yo' husband. Them hoes in Atlanta do all type of shit to get and keep a nigga attention, especially niggas from New Orleans," she said, and I instantly became sick to the stomach. Just the thought of Mahsyn touching kissing, caressing, or even thinking about giving another bitch what he gave me made me sick.

"Bitch, don't say that." My voice was stern but full of hurt.

"Well, boss the fuck up and go get yo' husband back. We all fuck up, some shit bigger than others, but we are all flawed, Zee. If this was a perfect fucking world, it wouldn't be fun. Nah go get yo' nigga, and I love you," she said.

"I love you more," I told her, and I laughed, hanging up the phone. I knew I had a lot of soul searching to do before I even saw Mahsyn, because I prayed and prayed and forgave myself, but my biggest fear was that he wouldn't forgive me. I jumped in my Benz and pulled off. I wasn't riding a full ten minutes when my phone rang. I was surprised that Mahyesha was calling me because I was sure she would take her son's side in the entire situation, because I hadn't talked to her since the ordeal at

Mhyia's funeral. I was scared to answer the phone because I wasn't in the mood to be disrespectful or disrespected. I connected my phone via Bluetooth before answering.

"Hello," I said, scared because I knew her mouth could be vicious.

"Girl, what took yo' ass so long to answer mem and where you staying at because I know yo' ass went back to New Orleans?" she asked me, and I smiled because she knew me so well. I heard crying in the background and instantly thought of my babies and began to cry. I was so caught up in my own personal shit that I forgot I was a mother first. I'd die before I repeated what my mother did to us.

"Is that my babies?" I asked through tears.

"They damn sure ain't mine," she laughed. "I'm not mad at you, Zenobia, because I understand what you went through, and that was a part of God's plan for y'all. I forgive you long as you forgive yourself. That's a conversation for another day. I called you because Mahsyn is in jail out here in Atlanta, but they are about to bring his dumbass down there talking about some murder charge that I ain't getting into over these phones." I understood her. "But I need you to put your big girl panties on and get ready to fight for your husband. I know it won't be easy, but you better be ready." I knew what she was speaking of, but something in her voice told me that it was more than just this murder shit. I didn't want to ask too much, so I let her talk. "You know New Orleans slow, so you need to call his lawyer to get him an early court date for a bond hearing," she said. "Nah go handle yo' business and let me tend to yo' rugrats," she said and disconnected the call before I could get a word in.

My mind was all over the place, and I had some questions that only Mahsyn could answer. Since it was still early when I got home, I called his lawyer and explained everything that Mahyesha told me, but he already knew, which didn't surprise me. He told me that Mahsyn would be in New Orleans by noon, and the earliest bond hearing would be three days from tomorrow. That only gave me enough time to get him clothes and shoes for court as well as boss myself up to look the part of his beautiful wife, because my gut told me shit was about to get ugly before it would be pretty again.

❦ 4 ❦

MAGNOLIA

"Did she hang up?" I asked my mother when I heard Chunky stop talking. I'd been quiet the entire time my mother talked to her.

"Well, if the fuck she didn't, she gon' hear yo' loud ass on the phone but yeah, she hung up," she answered, and I laughed. The sound of Chunky's voice always soothed a nigga's soul, so this time was no different. She was all I needed in this world outside of my kids, and I didn't have her. She was my everything, but she broke my fucking heart. Then thoughts of that night haunted me like a plague and all that sweet shit went out the window. How could the motherfucker that ripped my heart out my chest put it back where it belonged? She walking around this fucking world with my heart in her pocket and I didn't know how to get it back.

"You have to forgive yourself before you can forgive her, right?" Now she was about to be on her spiritual shit.

"You lucky I didn't tell her about the Dior bitch, but that's your fuck up to tell not mine," she griped, but it was true. I knew Chunky wasn't out here fucking on no nigga because she wasn't built like that, and here I was fucking on a bitch I didn't even know.

18

"I know, Ma, but how you know where she lay her head at and I don't?" I asked her, because Mahyesha's ass was like the channel six news.

"You know I run the city, stop playing with me, and I also know that Khency helped her find a place. You better hope I don't charter the jet and drop these kids off to her ass. They getting on the last nerve I have left. I can't even fuck my husband without Mhayce crying ass fucking it up. That lil' nigga need his maw titty milk, because this Enfamil not agreeing with his stomach, and Zheno keep asking about her," she told me, and I felt like shit. I knew in my heart I had to forgive Chunky, but I just didn't know how. I needed God and a praying congregation to help me on this one. Mahyesha explained to me what happened and even the bitch Dior helped me understand what Chunky was going through and how I missed the signs, so I guess we were both to blame.

"Don't get quiet, you know we only got 15 minutes on this damn phone, so speak up," Mahyesha told me, and I laughed.

"Ain't too much I can say over the phone, but once I'm out here I'll break everything down to you. I know I fucked up, but it can be fixed on all fronts." She knew what I meant.

"I sure hope so," she said, and we disconnected the phone call as the guards brought me back to my cell.

I was scheduled to be brought back to New Orleans to face charges of first-degree murder, and I had no idea how this shit would turn out. These bitches had me in a cell by myself because I was in for murder, which was a good thing, because the thoughts I was having, I would have killed an innocent cell mate, the irony. I sat back on my bunk and thought about how I ended up here. The words kept replaying in my mind: "you killed my daughter's husband." So, Fhendi was married and fucking my wife. That nigga deserved what the fuck I did. Fair exchange, no robberies, so I guess we even because I fucked his wife, but he ended up dead.

Dior didn't deserve that shit, though. I could tell she was a sweet woman. She almost had me under her fucking spell. I could never love her more than I loved my wife because Zenobia was a part of me. I couldn't explain my feelings for Dior. Maybe I loved her, but I wasn't in love with her. She caught me when I was mad and vulnerable. I couldn't say she took advantage of me because I was a willing participant, but she didn't have to bring a nigga to her house. She was lonely and I get it, because I was lonely too. Now that I knew her father was the opp, I would use that to my advantage. I needed Chunky to stay where the fuck she was and take my kids with her, because shit was about to shake in Atlanta, and I didn't need her or my kids around when the tables flipped.

I thought and wrecked my brain on who the fuck their CI could possibly be but came up empty. I knew I wouldn't get any sleep tonight because the fucking bed was hard and smelled like piss. I didn't get a chance to shower, so I still smelled like sex, and I was stressed. These motherfuckers didn't know I took medication, so my fucking mind and nerves were on edge. Felt like the fucking walls were closing in on a nigga. I thought of I went to sleep that I wouldn't wake up. I was tripping, but the minute a picture of Chunky came in my mind, I was at ease, and I hated that. I hated the effect she had on me when she did something so horrific and unforgiveable and had the potential to sabotage our marriage. It angered me even more that thoughts of her touch, the way her body felt next to mine when we slept at night, the way her body smelled like vanilla and her locs would tickle my face when she slept on top of me, calmed me. I laughed at the thought.

When I closed my eyes, I saw my baby girl laying in her casket looking like an angel, and my eyes popped back open and I became full of rage. I was battling demons that I prayed that God could help me get through, because I felt like I was fighting a losing battle. If I forgave Chunky for what she did, would it tarnish Mhyia's memory? I felt like I would be disrespecting my daughter if my life went on without her. We could have more kids, but none of them would ever replace her. Zenobia stopped her life. Stopped her from being what she could become before it could even start. That was a hard ass pill to swallow, and I wasn't sure I could ever forgive her for that. My heart could probably forgive her because it belonged to her, but my mind couldn't forget the images of what had taken place and had gotten us to this point. Things could never be the same between us because every time I would look at her, I would see my daughter and rage would run through my veins. I might end up killing her, and I would never forgive myself for that.

❧ 5 ❧

JADORE DIOR

"Do you think he killed your husband?" Jhewelz asked me as we took shots of D'ussé. I didn't know what time it was, but the sun was rising and we were still drinking.

When she first came in, I cried and cried and finally broke down and told her what was going on, but I couldn't mention names because of confidentiality. I have told her many stories and vice versa, but I never told her anyone's name. She let me get all my cries out and tell her the story before she gave me her honest opinion. We'd drank all the José Cuervo and were on our second bottle of D'ussé, and I still wasn't drunk but was a little tipsy.

"First of all, you shouldn't have fucked your patient." She pointed her finger in my face, and I laughed. "Second of all, you brought his ass all the way out here to the sticks and told him your secrets. Bitch, you love that nigga." She laughed, but she was telling the truth. I knew my father was trying to set Mahsyn up, but I didn't know the why. I would find out, though, because I knew my mother's weak ass knew. All she needed was a tea party, and she would spill all the tea.

In just a few days, I felt for Mahsyn what took forever for me to feel for Fhendi. I'd never throw dirt on my husband's name, but Mahsyn gave me what I yearned for in three days, what I had been begging Fhendi to give me for years: time and attention. Mahsyn was attentive and listened to everything I had to say and actually paid attention and participated in the conversation. Fhendi was a wonderful husband but at times, he could be so distant and not in tune with me that we were merely co-existing. Then there were times when he was the perfect husband and I was his entire world, but we had to get to that point of under-standing. With Mahsyn, it just came naturally. I didn't give a fuck if he was married or even if he forgave his wife and they got back together. I enjoyed the time we had while it lasted, I just didn't want him in jail for something that wasn't true.

"I do love him but when I look at him, I can still see that he is still in love with his wife," I told Jhewelz and threw a shot back. I didn't want him to leave his wife on my account because karma was a bitch.

"I forgot you said that nigga had a wife. Yeah, I wouldn't fuck with that. You are too beautiful to be any man's number two." We clicked our shot glasses together and threw them back.

"Not number twwooo," I dragged it out, and we laughed. I got up and went to the window and noticed the sun had come up.

"Bitch, I gotta go. I got four deliveries today and I'm here with yo' ass getting drunk," Jhewelz said as she stood to her feet on wobbly legs. She grabbed her purse and keys, making her way toward me, and kissed my cheek.

"Don't overthink shit. If it's meant to be, he'll be back. Trust me, they always come back." She hugged me, and I walked her to her car and watched as she pulled out my driveway. I knew she was good to drive because we'd gotten drunk as hell and she still managed to make it home, so this shit was no different.

Jason told me that they would be transporting Mahsyn to New Orleans at 10 a.m. and he had a court date in three days for a bond hearing. I had the rest of the week off, so I would be on a flight to New Orleans for that because I wanted him to know that I didn't believe that shit at all. I knew this would be tricky, but I needed Jhewelz with me, so the confidentiality shit went out the window once we got in the courtroom. Sleep wouldn't come easy because my thoughts were of him. I knew I couldn't have him to myself because his words shot daggers to my heart when he spoke them. They replayed over and over in my head like a broken record, and I couldn't shake them. I knew I wouldn't be able to sleep, so I connected my phone to my surround sound system and played the first song that came to mind.

You're everything I thought you never were
And nothing like I thought you could've been
But still you live inside of me
So tell me, how is that?
You're the only one I wish I could forget
The only one I love to not forgive
And though you break my heart
You're the only one
And though there are times when I hate you 'cause I can't erase
The times that you hurt me and put tears on my face
And even now while I hate you, it pains me to say
I know I'll be there at the end of the day
I don't wanna be without you, babe
I don't want a broken heart
Don't wanna take a breath without you, babe
I don't want to play that part
I know that I love you, but let me just say
I don't wanna love you in no kind of way, no, no
I don't want a broken heart
And I don't want to play the brokenhearted girl
No, no, no brokenhearted girl
I'm no brokenhearted girl

Beyoncé's "Brokenhearted Girl" flowed through my speakers as I let the beat work through my body. Her words described how I felt about Fhendi leaving me and Mahsyn being taken away. I moved my body like a snake then fell into a full split as I let my body display what my mouth couldn't speak to either one of them. My heart ached and soul cried as I thought about what my life had become. I regret the day Mahsyn walked into my office. I should have just given him his medication and let him walk away, but I thought I could fix his broken heart because it mirrored mine. I ended up losing more pieces of mine that I knew I couldn't get back, but I would try.

With my hands in the air. I stood on my toes like a ballerina and twirled until my body was sweaty and tired, but my mind couldn't rest. I was torn between chasing Mahsyn and letting the memory of Fhendi go, but I couldn't because I felt like he was somewhere in this world without me, and that pained me more than living this life without him. I hated him for leaving me but wanted him to come back to me. I wanted Mahsyn in my life, but I didn't want to be the reason he left his wife, because she didn't deserve that. I was once and still am in her shoes. I danced and danced until I cried until the song went off, and I fell to the floor in a fit of sobs. I had no one to help me fix me, but I was able to fix everyone else. After my five minutes of crying, I pulled myself together and went up my spiral staircase. There wasn't more I could do, so I dragged myself up the stairs hoping to get a little sleep before booking our flights to the Big Easy.

❧ 6 ❧
ZENOBIA

"**Y**ou coming to the mall with me or what?" I asked him over the phone as I jumped in my car. It was spring break so classes ended early, and I needed to get to the mall to get Mahsyn's clothes for court. I hadn't talked to him, but I knew he was in the city. Even from jail niggas knew he was back home.

Since I'd met MJ, it was like a breath of fresh air. He was someone I could talk to. I never thought about him sexually and he didn't either. We had an unspoken bond. We hadn't so much as kissed. He was just different but felt so familiar. At first he was on some fuck shit, trying to get me to his house, but after I shut that shit down, we been tight since. I looked at him more as a little brother anyway because he was so much younger than me. I had him by five years. There wasn't nothing his young ass could for me but give me a wet ass, and until I knew what was up with me and my husband, wasn't nobody touching this pussy. He knew I was married because I never took my ring off and never planned to. After the conversation I had with Mahyesha, Mahsyn had to know that I was coming hard behind him. He said the only way out of our marriage was toe tags and I stood ten toes on that. I forgave myself for what happened and now it was time for him to forgive us both so we could work on our marriage.

"Yeah, I'm coming, and don't be trying to boss a nigga around either. You holding your own shit today," he barked in the phone, and I laughed. He knew every time we went to the mall, he trailed behind me holding all my bags. This time would be no different.

MJ, because the nigga never told me his real name, was a handsome fella for a young girl, but he had all the potential to break bitches' hearts. He told me he would never tell me his real name because if he told me he would have to kill me, but I knew it was bullshit so I let him be. I would get looks from bitches, some would even whisper about us, and I would laugh when we were out. He said I would cock block but I wasn't. I wasn't holding his ass hostage. I would even offer to talk to the chicks for him, but he wasn't feeling it. He said he knew how to handle his business, so I backed off.

"If I want you to hold my shit then you holding my shit. Nah where you at so I can pull up?" He dropped his location and I headed to Algiers to pick him up.

The one thing I hated about MJ was that he was a dopeboy. Not just any Dopeboy, but he ran the blocks. I didn't want that for him. Over our many talks, I learned that he did graduate from high school with a 4.0 GPA but felt like college wasn't for him. His mother didn't push the issue and his father wasn't in the picture, so he went with his move in the drug game. I didn't ask too much because I knew he wouldn't tell me. He knew I was married and who I was married to, so it wasn't a big deal. I pulled up on Elmira and he was standing outside like he was waiting on me. I can't lie, dude was cute as fuck. Mocha-colored skin with dreads that hung in his face. His tall, muscular build would make any bitch trap him, but he was like a brother to me.

Today he was dressed in skinny jeans, Jordans, and a v-neck tee. His Hermes belt had his jeans hanging grown-man low with his gold chain around his neck. He was smiling and standing close to a female as she rubbed his arm. I watched as he threw his dreads back, displaying his grill, and the girl blushed. They looked cute, but I could tell he wasn't that interested in the girl. I waited for a few minutes before I blew my horn loud as fuck. He jumped like he had firecrackers under his ass and looked my way. Ole girl rolled her eyes like I gave a fuck, as he whispered something in her ear that made her blush before walking toward my car. He hopped in laughing, smelling like a loud pack, so I knew he was high.

"What's so damn funny?" I asked him as I pulled off.

"Yo' ass, bruh, you be hating." He looked at me with low eyes.

"No, I don't. Yo' ass was taking too long and I got shit to do," I told him as we got on the highway. We were going to the Mall of Louisiana to get Mahsyn's clothes.

"I know we going to get Magnolia's clothes. That nigga got court tomorrow, huh?" He looked at me stone faced.

"I know you not the one hating, nigga," I told him, trying not to take my eyes off the road.

"Nah, but the entire city know you that nigga wife. How that's gon' look with us walking around the mall together?" he asked me, and I laughed.

"Like we going to get his dumb ass some clothes and besides, you look like you could be my lil' brother." I laughed, but he didn't.

"Okay, but I'm telling you that nigga don't want no smoke." I laughed at him because we couldn't have been talking about the same nigga. If that's the case, MJ didn't want no smoke.

It took us about an hour to get the mall and find a parking space. We walked in and went straight to Macy's. I picked up Gucci shoes with the matching gray suit and tie and a white oxford shirt. I went to the women's section and picked out a gray Gucci peplum dress to match him, and I already had my red bottoms at home. I had an appointment with my stylist to retwist and crinkle my locs for me. We were walking to the counter when I heard a familiar voice. I grabbed MJ by his collar so we could hide in the coat rack.

"The fuck, Nobby!" he yelled, and I tried to cover his mouth with my hand.

"That's Magnolia's ex-wife. I thought this bitch was dead," I whispered to him, because I thought she was. Last I heard, she dropped off the face of the earth taking the twins with her. I wasn't hiding from her but whoever she was on the phone with, she was spilling some hot fucking tea, and I didn't want her to see me and stop talking. Our two grown asses were in between the clothing racks a few feet away from where she was yapping her fucking gums. She couldn't see us, but I could damn sure see her. MJ got up.

"Man, this bitch don't know me. You can hide and listen, but I'm going to pay for this shit because I'm hungry and ready to go." I went into my purse to give him my card, but he stopped me.

"Nah, I got this, but you gon' pay for our food." He smiled and stood to his feet and carried all the clothes to the counter.

Her was right. MJ walked past Candyce and she didn't stop talking. She didn't even look his way, and I was glad. I looked down and noticed four little feet, so I knew she had the twins with her. I peeked my head too far out and Janae saw me. She ran full speed toward me, jumping in my arms, knocking us both to the floor. Candyce was so busy on the fucking phone that she didn't even notice Janae running off.

"I miss you, Nobby, I wanna come wit' you," she whined with one arm around my neck and her thumb in her mouth with the other. "Where's my daddy?" she asked me, laying her head on my shoulder. "Mommy said he left us, and I don't like living with Mommy. Pwease take me with you." Bad as I wanted to take the twins, I couldn't.

"Shhhhh, I need you to go back to your mommy and act like

you never saw me, okay, and I promise I'll come steal you from your mommy. You and your sister, okay." I held out my pinky for her to take. We pinky promised on it and she ran back to Candyce, wrapping her arms around her mother's leg, never breaking eye contact with me.

"Yeah, he was fucking some doctor bitch in Atlanta and got caught up in some murder charge for killing Fhendi, but I'm about to get the fuck soon as I get my money. The feds giving me quarter a mil to leave town and I'm taking my girls with me. He could raise him and that bitch kids since he forgot about the two we have." She paused as to listen to whoever was on the other end of the phone. I peeked and noticed MJ stupid ass listening in too. He was playing with the rack with the socks and she was on the other side. "Bitch, I don't care what the fuck happens to him. He said fuck me so I'm about to fuck him." She laughed into the phone and hung up. She didn't even buy shit. She grabbed the twins hands in a hurry and walked to the exit.

"Get yo' silly ass up, hiding like a damn child." MJ laughed at me as I stood to my feet. This bitch made a deal wit' the devil, but how the fuck did she get that type of info on Mahsyn? Of course, I knew what the fuck happened to Fhendi, but who the fuck told her? This bitch had to go.

"This bitch working with the feds, Nobby. How you gon' handle this shit?" MJ asked as he threw the suit bag over his shoulder.

"I'll handle that bitch later." I didn't want to tell him my plans because what happened between me and my husband was between him and me.

"Well, now that we got the clothes we can go, because I got a taste for seafood and after the racks I dropped on some shit that ain't even for me, we going to Fiery Crab on your dime." I laughed at him because I knew he was about to fuck up some commas on food. My phone ringing jarred me from my thoughts. I noticed it was Mahyesha calling.

"What's up, Ma?" I took my phone off Bluetooth so MJ

couldn't hear what she said. MJ was my potnah, but I didn't trust anyone when it came to my family.

"They pushed Mahsyn's court date back a week and he is pissed. I told him how slow New Orleans was, but don't worry about a bond because they ain't got shit to hold him. We gon' fly in the night before. Did you get his clothes?" she asked me, and I answered.

"Yeah, I got everything, and guess who I saw in the mall?" I told her.

"Who?" she asked.

"Candyce," I told her, and the phone got silent.

"I thought that bitch was dead. Did she have my grandbabies with her?" Mahyesha asked me.

"Yeah, and Janae saw me. She kept saying that she wanted to come live with me because she didn't like Candyce." I thought back to when my brother was killed. My mind kept telling me that they ended Candyce too, unless this bitch had nine lives. Miss Jazzie fucking my mind up with this shit, because this bitch just popping up out of nowhere. I knew she was up to something, but I just don't know what yet.

"You know you gotta make shit shake right and get those girls. You gotta get on that shit ASAP. You need me to call somebody to assist you? Did she see you?" Mahyesha asked me, but I didn't need the help. She should know by now that my lady nuts were big as fuck, and I could handle this shit without the Masons being involved.

"Nah, she ain't see me, but I got some shit I need to run by you when y'all touch down that ain't pretty." I looked over at MJ who was knocked out on the passenger side. I really loved this lil' nigga like a brother. I had to tell Mahyesha what Candyce said, but not over the phone lines because I didn't trust them.

"Well, you got enough time to do what you need to do in time for his court date, and who is that lil' nigga you got with you everywhere you go?" My mouth formed a big O because Mahyesha knew every fucking thing.

"Oh, New Orleans is my city, so I know everything that happens in it. I know you ain't fucking with him like that, so you can keep ya lil' friend, but be mindful of how Mahsyn is behind you," she fussed, and I was lost for words.

"It's not like that. He's like a brother to me," I told her when I found my voice.

"Oh, I know, but I also know that y'all been spending a lot of time together, but keep it friendly, Nobby," she told me, and I agreed.

"I'll see you when we touch down, and you getting these badass boys soon as we touch down because me and my husband need some alone time," she told me before hanging up, and I got excited. It had been almost a month since I saw my babies, and I missed them. After I left Atlanta, Mahsyn cut all contact with me. He blocked me from calling and completely shut me out like I wasn't his wife, but now I see why. He had a new bitch he was fucking on, and I hoped I ran into her because it was definitely up for that bitch. I knew he told her he was married, so I might just go upside his fucking head for playing with me too. I pulled up to Fiery Crab and parked the car.

"Wake yo' hungry ass up." I pushed MJ's shoulder, and his red eyes shot to mine angrily.

"You drive so fucking slow I thought we would never make it," he said, and I laughed.

"No, you just need to stop smoking so much weed," I told him.

"Maybe you should smoke a blunt or two and loosen yo' ass up." We laughed as we got out the car to eat some good ass seafood.

After feeding our faces, I decided to take MJ up on his offer and put one in the air with him. He rolled three blunts as I drove back to my condo. Once we were inside and situated, I went to take a shower as he got comfortable in front the TV. I put on my boy shorts and t-shirt and joined him. My ass had gotten bigger in the last month because I still was trying to lose the baby weight from the twins, but I was almost there. I had about 20 more pounds to lose, but I was comfortable in my skin. I swung my dreads to one side and flopped down next to MJ. This was a ritual for us, but this time I would smoke with him. I usually had my french vanilla Stella Rosa wine and we binge watched shit on Netflix. Tonight was no different. He looked over at me, giving me a twice over, and laughed.

"Don't start that shit, I wear this all the time," I told him, and he smirked.

"But you big ole fine, and I'm a fucking man. You know I don't look at you like that, but it's hard not to when you walk around this bitch with yo' ass hanging out. I'm a man with a dick at the end of the day, Nobby." He laughed, and I couldn't help but agree. I tucked my thighs under me as far as they could go and took the blunt from him. I inhaled smoke through my mouth, letting it flow through my nose before blowing it out. This shit felt so familiar. Like the first time I smoked with Mahsyn. It was definitely déjà vu. My head fell back onto the sofa and I laughed.

"What's funny?" he asked as I passed him the blunt, looking at him.

"This is exactly how I fell in love with my husband," I told him, and it was his turn to laugh.

"Only he was the one to pop my cherry." My smile fell and so did his when my words registered in his head.

"Damn, so he the only nigga that touched the pussy?" he asked, licking his lips.

"Of course, and will continue to be the only nigga." We both bust out laughing. The effects of the weed had me feeling good as hell. I stretched out across the sofa with my head in his lap. I felt his dreads brush my face as he lifted mine so I could get comfortable.

"Fuck no, I ain't stepping on Magnolia toes. I heard 'bout what that nigga capable of, and I ain't trying to get in his way. I can control myself. I ain't trying to die." I laughed because Mahsyn was a gentle giant, or at least he used to be.

"We just be vibing, MJ, and this is my way to keep yo' ass safe. When you here, I know you not out fucking up the streets. You're safe here." I looked up at him, and he grinned. It caught me off guard because he looked so familiar. Maybe it was the weed. I had to be tripping.

"Good looking out, though. I like the fact that you look out for me, because nobody else does. My momma doing her own thing and I told you 'bout my pops. It's good to know you care about me enough to protect me, because I didn't have that shit growing up," he said, and I sat up to look at him.

"What's up? Talk to me," I told him.

"Man, my momma was so bitter when my pops left her. The funny thing is, she hates me because she said that I look so much like him. She said he wanted her to abort me because they were so young, and he wasn't ready for a baby and neither was she. He gave her the money but instead of her going through with the abortion, she saved the money while going to school, got a job and saved. By the time she had me, my dad was in the wind and she was left to raise me. I didn't make her bitter but my father did," he said, and I felt sorry for him. I knew what it felt like to be a fatherless child.

"Well, don't worry about the past, just know you got me," I told him and patted his shoulder.

"Even when that nigga Magnolia walk in this bitch? Because you gotta know he coming," he said, and I laughed.

"If and when he comes, he ain't got a choice but to accept you because you were there for me when he wasn't." I kissed his cheek and laid back down as we watched *Queen of the South* on Netflix.

❧ 7 ❧

JADORE DIOR

My father told me that they pushed Mahsyn's court hearing for a week, so that gave me time to prepare myself to see him again. Jason told me not to go to New Orleans because Mahsyn was a married man, but I didn't care. I knew there was a chance that his wife and kids would be there, but I'd cross that bridge when I got to it. I had the right to explain that I had nothing to do with why he was arrested. Yes, Jason was my father, but that was more of his doing than mine. I would never put him in a compromising position because he was my patient. Not only that, but I was feeling him. He had to know that I was in no way connected to his wife. I didn't even know who she was. Whether my father wanted me to or not, I was going to New Orleans. I'd booked our flights and hotel rooms, so I had a day to prepare. I picked up my phone to call Jhewelz to make sure she didn't flake on me at the last minute.

"Bitch, don't call me trying to see if I'm still coming, because I am. I got one more delivery then I'm heading yo' way. My shit already packed," she answered on the first ring. "I still don't understand why you feel the need to plead your case to a married man. He gon' believe what he wanna believe anyway. I hope you are prepared to see his wife, because she is definitely going to be there, so you gotta be ready if he don't choose you." Sometimes I hated that she was bluntly honest, but she was telling the truth.

"I thought about all that, but I need to tell him that I didn't have nothing to do with him being arrested," I spoke into the phone.

"When you think about it, Dior, you do, because Jason is your father. He played a big part. Think about it, outside of me, your father is the only man that knows where you live and everything about you. You don't think that nigga put all that together while he sitting in that fucking cell? You walking in hot water, Dior, and I don't want you to get burned," she said.

"I'm a big girl. I can take whatever he throwing, but he will know my side of the story," I told her and hung up the phone.

While I waited on her to arrive, I made sure I'd packed everything I needed for our trip. I knew I wanted to do some sightseeing, so we were leaving a few days early. I didn't know what to expect, so I packed for every occasion and weather forecast. Once everything was ready, I grabbed my glass and poured my wine and waited for Jhewelz to show up.

"Damn, you just couldn't wait, huh?" Jhewelz walked in my door looking like new money. She had on her red fedora hat with her tube sundress and Gucci sandals. Her huge Gucci shades hid her eyes as she smiled at me. I had to look down at myself and cringed. I had on a plain white t-shirt and jeans with boots.

"Oh no, we going to New Orleans. I need you to be dressed better than that." She grabbed me to my feet. "Plus, we don't know what we walking into with these New Orleans bitches, let's go." She dragged me upstairs to change my clothes.

When we came back downstairs, I was dressed in a skintight Dior red mini dress that hugged every curve God gave me. On my feet were tan sandals that wrapped up my thick calves and thighs. This bitch had me looking like I was about to rip the runway.

"Now that's better. You trying to be in the city that never sleeps looking like Grandma Sooky instead of the bad bitch you are. We leaving titles in Georgia, sweetie, and displaying our big ass Georgia peaches." We laughed as she grabbed her wine glass. I felt sexy as hell. I hadn't dressed like this since the last trip Fhendi and I went on to Aruba.

"We not carrying shit. I got a driver and crew to carry all our shit and wait on us hand and foot, so let's go," she said, and we walked out the door hand in hand to the airport.

I couldn't help the dragonflies that jumped around inside my stomach when we landed. The excitement of the unknown scared me a little. We stepped off the airplane and entered the lobby. We went to sit and wait for our luggage to come when my legs were attacked by little arms wrapping around them.

"My mommy," I heard the little boy say, squeezing my legs tighter. I had to balance myself so I wouldn't fall in the seat.

"Zheno, bring yo' ass here, boy," I heard a lady's voice yell from across the lobby. I looked up into a lady's eyes as I tried to unhook his arms from around my legs.

"No, sweet face, I'm not your mommy," I told him, rubbing my hand through his beautiful hair.

"Girl he been running through here looking for his momma because he know we about to see her. I'm sorry about that." Her accent was strong, so I knew she was from here.

"Oh, it's okay, ma'am." I smiled because the little boy was too cute and handsome. He looked up at me and his light-colored eyes looked familiar. I wanted to call out to Jhewelz to see his eyes, but she must have run off to the bathroom.

"Mahyesha, his lil' ass ran off again? I told you we should have taken the jet," I heard a deep baritone voice call out to the lady trying to pry the lil' boy from my legs. I looked up into the eyes of the most beautiful creature that graced this earth. His beautiful hair was in a bun, he had a broad chest, enticing slanted eyes, and bow legs.

"Watch ya eyes, little girl, that's my husband," the lady

Mahyesha said, and I felt offended. "Don't get offended, baby, my husband gets those looks all the time, but I'll kill a bitch behind that one."

I heard the man laugh, but my eyes never left hers. She wasn't playing. He walked up behind her and wrapped one of his arms around her waist, pulling her to her feet. It was then I noticed the man holding a baby carrier. I was trying to be nosy and see the baby, but I couldn't because the top was covered.

"That's not Mommy, Zheno, you gon' see her soon." The man grabbed at lil' man, and he let me go. I was glad, because this lady was about to beat my ass for looking at her husband. I didn't disrespect my elders, but I wasn't gon' let her beat my ass either.

"Again, sorry about that," she said before her and her little family walked away from me.

"What the fuck was that all about?" Jhewelz walked up to me.

"I don't know. The little boy thought I was his momma. It was weird though." I shrugged my shoulders and went to get our luggage.

✤ 8 ✤

MAGNOLIA

I knew they would set my hearing back a week, but I wasn't tripping. They just wanted me in jail a little while longer. The system needed that time to build a case because they didn't have shit on me. I met with my lawyer once and found out that wasn't even Fhendi's body. He also stated that Det. Jason was on my head behind some beef shit with the old head Masons that didn't have shit to do with me. I respected that, though, because we moved as a unit and executed as a unit as well.

I needed these past few days to reflect on some shit that had been heavy on my mind. From my marriage to this feeling I couldn't describe for Dior. I craved her. I wasn't in love with her, but I had a need for her to be in my life, if that makes sense. Even though I was the cause of her pain, I somehow felt obligated to fill that void for her. If she knew her husband was never coming back, it would break her. I heard the pain and hurt in her voice when she opened up to me. But to know that her father had a hand in my arrest threw me for a loop. I knew I couldn't fuck with Dior, but I could fuck her mind, and that's what I planned to do when I got out of here. I knew it would hurt Chunky if she showed up, but she showed me her decision when she killed my fucking daughter. All bets were off.

My mind was conflicted. I couldn't decipher if my feelings for her were genuine or out of guilt for what I'd done. Then there was Zenobia, my everything, my all, my endgame. I knew I shouldn't still be in love with her, but she was my person, my medicine, my light in this dark ass world. I never thought of living my life without her once we were married but now, I didn't think I could look her in the eyes. Shit was weird. How could I still be in love with the woman who killed our seed? Love didn't conquer all, and I couldn't just forgive her and act like the shit didn't happen. Life didn't work like that. I'd killed niggas for less than that in the streets. It pained me for what she did, but I knew I had to forgive her for my own peace of mind and to move forward.

I'd taken my shower already and one of the guards brought my clothes to me. I took one look at the outfit and knew Chunky got this for me. I smiled because even though I hated her, she still came through for a nigga. I slipped into my clothes and waited for the guard to call me for court.

"Calvary," the guard yelled my name, and I wanted to hit him in his shit. I walked to the door and stuck my wrists through the hole so they could cuff me. Once the doors were open, they shackled my ankles and took me down to the courtroom.

Before I got to my seat, my eyes scanned the courtroom, and the first face I saw was Dior with Jhewelz sitting next to her. That fucked me up because I didn't know they were fucking friends. Dior was looking good as fuck from what I could see. The tan color she had on fit her doctor mentality very well. She was sitting on the opposite side, which meant she wasn't here for me, she was here for her dead ass husband. That infuriated me more, but I couldn't show it. Whatever her paw told her, she must have believed.

My eyes went behind me and I saw Mahyesha, Ghiani, and Zenobia. She had on a gray dress to match my suit. She was holding my son and my heart broke. To the side of her were Zheno, Janae, and Monae. How the fuck did she get the twins? I didn't even know she knew where they were. When we moved to ATL, I searched high and low for Candyce's ass but I couldn't find her, but clearly I wasn't looking hard enough because Chunky found her. I looked at Zenobia for any type of emotion, but she showed none as she rocked our son. Her eyes never left mine, but I could see the hurt in them. I followed her eyes as she looked at Dior and Jhewelz and knew she wanted to buck because she felt betrayed. I knew Chunky like I knew the back of my fucking hand, and she felt played. If we weren't in the courtroom, she would probably beat the fuck out of both of them. Her eyes met mine again, and her nostrils flared. She was angry hurt. She wanted to fuck some shit up but out of respect for our family, she swallowed that shit like she swallowed my nut. I was proud of her for keeping her poker face on full display, but I knew once this shit was over, it was lights out for Dior and Jhewelz. Chunky probably thought I had something to do with that shit, but I was just as shocked as she was. I felt fucking played, but I would get the answers I needed.

"All rise for the Honorable Judge Dewitt," the bailiff said, and everybody stood up.

After we sat down, the prosecutor tried to show the pictures of the dead body from Atlanta to the judge, but my lawyer was already on it. They even tried to say that they had a CI that put me at the scene of the crime but they couldn't get in touch with the CI for court. The judge released me on a 80k bond that was already paid. Once the handcuffs came off, I went straight to my kids. I took Mhayce from Zenobia and the rest of my kids gathered around me, hugging my legs. That shit felt so good. I hated being away from them, but I had some other shit to address. I handed Mhayce back to Zenobia without making eye contact. I turned around and watched as Dior and her friend tried to rush out the door, but one of my men stopped them. I turned to walk away and I heard Zenobia's voice.

"You're welcome." I turned to her and finally looked in her pain-filled eyes.

"The fuck am I thanking you for?" It came out harsh, but I meant what I said.

"Those clothes you got on. I bought that shit and I bonded your ass out of jail, but you 'bout to run behind yo' hoe. Don't think I didn't see that bitch Jhewelz run out this bitch," she said and walked into my personal space so that only she and I could hear.

"I am yo' fucking wife first and when you down, I will always have your fucking back, but what you won't do is disrespect me for a bitch that don't know fuck about you. I won't beg for your forgiveness, you'll give it to me when you ready, but my life doesn't fucking stop because you wanna be childish and fuck a bitch because you mad. I am your medicine, nigga." She grabbed my hard dick with her free hand. "That bitch could never give you what I give you." She let my shit go and grabbed Zheno's hand, who in turn grabbed his sisters' hands. "Move the fuck out the way so the queen can pass, nigga." Her eyebrow went up, and I moved out her way to let her pass. I couldn't say shit because everything she said was right.

"And that's my fucking daughter and her word is law," Mahyesha said before Ghiani grabbed her messy ass up. "And that's on period. Don't leave your 80 for the fucking 20," she said and walked behind Zenobia out the courtroom. My dick was still hard from how Chunky bossed up on my ass, but I wouldn't expect anything but boss shit from her.

❧ 9 ❧
JADORE DIOR

"Hold the fuck up, where you think you going?!" I heard behind me as I dragged Jhewelz because her ass was walking too slow.

"Why the fuck you didn't tell me you were fucking Zenobia's husband, Dior?!" She stopped walking and looked at me. We could discuss whatever she wanted to discuss once we got the fuck away from here, because Mahsyn was mad and I didn't want to be on the receiving end of it.

"Who the fuck is Zenobia, bitch?" I asked her as we power walked to the car. It looked like the closer we got the further the fucking car was.

"Motherfucker, I said stop." I heard Mahsyn's voice getting closer and wanted to take off running, but these heels would fail me.

"Magnolia's wife, Dior, the fuck were you thinking?" she asked me, but before I could answer her I felt my body being yanked backward.

"So you knew all along, huh?" Mahsyn asked me but was looking at Jhewelz.

"Mahsyn, Dior is my best friend, so no, I didn't know she was fucking you. She don't discuss her patients with me," she told Mahsyn, and that was a lie.

"How the fuck you knew I was her patient then, bitch?" he asked her, and I stepped in.

"Aim the disrespect at me not my friend. She didn't know who you were because I didn't discuss you. She only came with me for moral support. I only came to tell you the real truth about what the fuck was going on.

"So you mean to tell me that you didn't know your best fucking friend and my wife were friends?" he asked me.

"No, I didn't," I told him honestly. I thought back to the airport when I saw that lil' boy hugging my legs.

"Oh my god!" I covered my mouth with my hands. "That was your mother and kids I saw at the airport. He thought I was his mommy," I said more to myself but a little too loud.

"The fuck are you talking about?" he asked me, and I ran down the entire scene to him. He ran his hands over his beard and backed away from me.

"You fucking with me right now, right? How the fuck I know you not working with yo' daddy trying to pin me for your husband's murder?" he told me, and that stung. That was a shot to the chest.

"Hold up, Mahsyn." That was Jhewelz trying to defend me, but he pushed her hand from his chest.

"This ain't got shit to do with you, right?" She shook her head from left to right fast as fuck. "Mind ya fucking business then," he finished and looked back at me.

"Answer my fucking question." He pressed my body against the rental car we had. The heat from his body and looking at the scowl on his face turned me on. I wanted to caress his cheek ad kiss his lips, but now wasn't the time for that. His hand gripped the front of my neck, pushing me further into the car.

"I didn't have anything to do with whatever my father is trying to do, I swear. Everything I told you and feel for you is real. Why would I lie to you? I didn't even know you before you walked into my office," I pleaded with him as I tried to pry his hand from my throat. He was cutting my air supply and I felt faint.

"My fucking husband is not dead!" I screamed, because I was losing it. I refused to believe that shit.

"Why the fuck is your father trying me like I won't fuck him up?" he asked me, but I didn't have an answer for him.

"I don't know, Mahsyn, I promise." I tried to wrap my arms around his neck, but he pushed me away. Another jab at my heart. He let my neck go and looked at Jhewelz.

"You a snake ass bitch. You knew what we went through, even came to my daughter's fucking funeral, and you went with yo' move like this?" He backed away from me and turned to her.

"I told you before that she does not discuss her patients with me, so how was I supposed to know that she was fucking with you? I didn't even know you were one of her patients until now." She was telling half the truth because I told her the situation, but I never mentioned names. He stared at her hard for a few minutes before he backed up and started to walk away.

"Please, Mahsyn, don't leave!" I yelled behind him because I needed him. My voice fell on deaf ears because he kept walking until he got into the passenger side of a G wagon and they pulled off. Jhewelz grabbed my shoulder and pulled me into a hug as I cried.

"Don't ever beg a nigga for what you don't deserve." She hugged me tighter as I mulled over her words and sobbed harder.

🦋 10 🦋

MAGNOLIA

"**W**hat the fuck do we know?" I asked Ghiani as we pulled off and he handed me the blunt.

I didn't have time to pacify anybody's feelings. I needed to find out who was running their fucking mouth. Mahyesha rode with Chunky and the kids, and Ghiani waited for me because I needed some information that only he knew how to get.

"Ole girl back there telling the truth. She really don't fuck with her parents like that, so whatever bullshit Jason on, it's personal. He hated Fhendi, but he using that shit to try and sink you," he said as we weaved through traffic.

"Who the fuck is the CI?" I thought out loud. We had to find whoever that was before my next court date or I was facing football numbers.

"That I don't know. Whoever it is, they hiding that motherfucker good but don't worry, I got somebody on it. I'll know in a week," Ghiani said, giving me a strange look.

"What nigga?" I asked him, giving the blunt back.

"That ain't the only shit I found when I was digging in the ground." I couldn't take any more bullshit. He hit the blunt once and gave it back to me.

"You gon' need this bitch more than me for what I'm about to tell you," he said, and that piqued my antennae.

"I spoke with Endymion the other day, and the nigga that's fucking with our numbers is Mariah's son," he told me, and I choked on the smoke.

"What fucking Mariah?" I said through the coughs, and he gave me a knowing look.

"Yo' first love, motherfucker," he said, and I pulled hard as fuck on the blunt and kept the smoke in my lungs. I needed something strong as fuck to talk about that fucking memory.

"Nigga, I need a fucking drink," I told him.

"Say less, nigga," Ghiani said as we hit the interstate in search of a bar that was open at 12 in the afternoon.

Mariah was the first woman I ever fucked with hard before I met Chunky. It was years before her on some puppy love type shit. We went to the same high school, and y'all know how that go. I was a popular hood nigga and she was hood royalty. Everybody wanted to be us on the Eastbank. We were addicted to each other but toxic as fuck. If she saw me talking to another bitch, it was up for me and the bitch I was talking to and vice versa. She couldn't even look at another nigga. We thought we were in love, or at least thought we knew what love was. Her parents didn't want her with me, and that only made her cling to me more and I ate that shit up, turned her ass out. I had her mind and her heart, but she only had my mind. One fuck up and she got pregnant. We were both seniors in high school on our way to separate colleges. I was making money and didn't have time for hustling, school, and a fucking baby, so I gave her the money to get rid of it. She was heartbroken and felt like I abandoned her because I wanted her to kill something that was made out of love. I wasn't trying to hear that shit because we were both too young and Mahyesha wasn't having it. We went our separate ways, and I never heard from her again.

"Nigga, get out the car, we here." I looked up and we were at some upscale bar. I ain't give a fuck long as they had something strong.

We walked in and it was quiet, only a few people scattered around, but I needed a drink.

"Let's grab a table in the corner," Ghiani said, and I followed him to a table in the corner. As we got closer, I noticed a woman with her back to us sitting at the table sipping a glass of wine. I stopped in my tracks because I knew who it was. Ghiani was trying to make me flash the fuck out. This was too fucking much in one day, and I needed to refresh and start again tomorrow.

"Nah nigga, don't stop now, this needs to happen." Ghiani pushed me and if I had a fucking gun, I would have killed his ass.

"Mariah." Her name slid off my tongue, and she turned her head to the sound of her name.

Her face hadn't changed a bit. Mocha-colored skin so smooth like it could be painted on canvas. Her hair was still long and she still had the most mesmerizing gray eyes since the day I met her. She stood to greet me, and she was still short as fuck, but her hips and ass had spread over the years, nice and plump. She was stacked on stacked. Her soft manicured hands were on her hips as we took each other in.

"Mahsyn." She smiled and closed the space between us and pulled me in for a hug. She still smelled like vanilla, just like Chunky. I almost got lost in the hug, but I let her go so we could talk.

"Mahsyn, I'm sorry, but I just couldn't kill our baby, but now he is wreaking havoc on the streets. I stay in New York but I had to come to the city because he is dipping in places that could get him killed," she said, and I was still fucked up about her having our kid. I had a fucking son out here that I knew nothing about. She talked about it like I was supposed to fix shit when I didn't even know what the lil' nigga looked like. I was trying not to hurt her feelings because I had more pressing shit to tend to.

"And what the fuck you expect me to do, Mariah? The nigga

probably don't even know about me," I told her, and her eyes lowered, giving me my answer.

"Where the fuck did you tell him his father was?" I felt the heat radiating from my face.

"I told him his daddy left us," she said, looking into my eyes. "I explained everything to him, Mahsyn. I wasn't going to lie to him," she said, and I wanted to smack the fuck out of her. She didn't even look the same to me as when I walked in. She looked evil. I knew I deserved everything she was saying, but she was being vindictive. I read body language very well. She did that so he would resent me if we ever crossed paths, and I didn't respect her for that.

"You right, I did leave, and I didn't want a child because we were on two different paths in life, but you had to know that this day would come, you vindictive bitch." My hands trembled, and Ghiani stepped toward the table.

"I can't do this shit anymore, Mahsyn. I tried to get him to come back to New York but he wants to run the streets. It's your turn," she told me, and I wanted to jump across the table.

"Don't fuck with it, Magnolia. I brought you here because I wanted you to hear it from the horse's mouth. It's time to go," he told me, but I didn't move. My body felt numb, Novocain numb. I stared at her with ill intent, because she had already painted the picture of me in his head, so I knew he hated me.

"What the fuck is his name, bitch?" I was done with respecting her, because she didn't deserve it. She grabbed her purse and stood from the table.

"Mahsyn Jr., but the streets call him MJ." She walked off without looking back, and if she knew what was best for her, she wouldn't come back.

❧ II ❧

ZENOBIA

After I dropped Mahyesha off at the hotel, I told her I would keep my kids so she could have some time with her husband. She deserved it. I knew Mahsyn would be surprised when he saw the twins, but how I got them was a totally different story. I was always the quiet, timid, and shy Zenobia, but that shit changed the minute I realized Candyce was playing with my husband. I ain't give a fuck who he was fucking and sucking, when you played with his fucking freedom, that brought another level of crazy out of me.

After that night with MJ, he left the next morning and I called Khency. I told her the situation and she told me that Endymion would handle it. Two days later, Khency was at my door with the twins. She told me that they had Candyce in the dungeon and to tell Mahsyn they would keep her there until he gave the okay to finish her. I didn't feel bad for what I did, but I did feel disrespected when he ran behind that bitch after court. I wanted that bitch canceled immediately, and if Mahsyn took too long to find me, I would kill that bitch my fucking self.

I told MJ to order pizza and wings for the kids, Mhayce's chunky ass would get breast milk, and to meet me at the house. I could only imagine the look on his face when he saw all my kids, but if he had a problem with it he could just leave. I pulled up to my parking spot and noticed MJ sitting in his truck on the phone. I blew my horn, getting his attention. He jumped and ended his call. He jumped out the car and practically ran to the driver side of my car.

"Damn, you brought the party home with you, huh?" He laughed and looked at the backseat at the kids. "I ordered the pizza but look like I need to order more." He nodded his head toward the sleeping twins and Zheno.

"How much did you order?" I asked him as I got out my car.

"Three pizzas and 25 wings, but you know yo' ass is greedy. You eat a whole pizza on your own." He laughed and I pushed him, but he was right. Pizza Hut meat lovers was my shit.

"It should be delivered in the next ten minutes. Let's get the kids out the car and into the house," he said and shocked the shit out of me. Of course, he knew I had kids but he'd never met them. He pulled the front seat forward and grabbed Zheno effortlessly, like he'd done it before. He gently tapped the twins and they woke up and got out the car. Janae put her thumb in her mouth and grabbed the loop on his jeans, as did Monae on the opposite side. He stood with Zheno over his shoulder and looked at me.

"You gon' get lil' man out the car seat? 'Cuz, umm, I ain't got no more hands." He looked at me as I stared at him in awe. I was stuck for a minute because I'd never witnessed him with kids but then again, he was an only child.

"Oh yeah, my bad." I grabbed Mhayce and his bag as we walked to the elevator. I wished I could take my phone out and capture this moment. Zheno over his shoulder and the twins walking with him with their little hands holding his belt loop on each side. It felt familiar. It gave me a sense of peace.

"Come on before the elevator close, Nobby, you daydreaming and shit." He laughed as I hurried to get on.

"MJ, you are full of surprises, my nigga. I thought you would take one look at all my kids and run for the fucking hills," I told him as the elevator started to move.

"Nah, I knew yo' kids would come one day with that nigga Magnolia being in jail, plus I like kids anyway, especially cute ones. You really care about a nigga, Nobby, and I appreciate that. I know yo' ass ain't old enough to be my mother, but a big sister would suffice." He reached over and kissed my cheek, and I blushed. I don't know why God blew him my way, but I was glad he did. I needed to check on Zyrese. He'd been with Jahari and Amerika because of school, but I didn't want him to feel neglected through all of this. I also didn't want him to be a part of this turmoil. I knew they were taking good care of him, so I wasn't tripping, but I did miss him. I made a mental note to have him spend the summer when the dust settled, because I was nowhere near settled. I just lived day by day.

Once we got the kids inside, MJ went back to my trunk to get the kids' clothes. Mahyesha had a lot of shit for them, and I had Khency get the twins everything they needed. I needed to reach out to her about the Candyce situation too, because Mahsyn had been in the wind since we left the courthouse. If we waited much longer, the bitch would become maggot food.

When he brought their stuff back up, I got out their PJs and got them ready for bed while MJ held Mhayce for me. He paced the floor, rocking Mhayce with his phone cradled to his ear. When I first met him, I thought he was so fucking sexy and wanted to fuck him, but the more time we spent together talking and doing different things, I realized I was glad we didn't take it there because that's not what he needed. He had enough hoes on his roster to give him everything he needed physically. I was there for him emotionally because our talks sometimes became intense, especially when he talked about his mother. He didn't have anything bad to stay about her, but she did make him feel neglected. He broke down the story his mother told him, and I cried because his mother was suffering from a broken heart. How could the man you loved tell you to abort your child?

I would have killed Mahsyn if he came at me with some shit like that.

"What yo' ass over there thinking so hard about?" MJ broke my thoughts, standing in front of me with Mhayce in his arms.

"I was just thinking about what you told me about your mother. Where is she?" I asked him.

"She lives in New York and works as a pharmacist. She hates what I do for a living. She thinks I'm a menace, but I'm not. I may have stepped on a couple of toes, but that ain't 'bout shit. I make my money and stay out the way for the most part, and being here with you got me losing money, but it's also sparing my life, so I appreciate it." He smiled at me. "Plus, you easy as hell to talk to. All these hoes want is dick, because they ain't getting a dolla outta me." I laughed.

"Let me take a quick shower in my bathroom, and you get comfortable too, because you ain't leaving no time soon," I told him and turned to leave and go to my room. He usually brought his hoe bag inside, so I knew it was somewhere around here. I walked away from him to my room while the kids played with their iPad.

I pulled out my typical boy shorts and t-shirt and hopped in the shower. I tried to put my locs in a bun, but they were so long that I knew some were going to get wet, but I didn't care. The hot water cascaded down my body as thoughts of Magnolia filled my mind. It angered me that he didn't acknowledge me and my loyalty to him. All that vanished when thoughts crept about how he caressed my body, leaving no spot untouched. The way my pussy purred with anticipation of his death stroke. I missed the way his tongue flicked at my nipples while we made love. The way he gripped my dreads while fucking me from the back with me looking back at him. He would look down at our connected bodies and bite his bottom lip. Shit was so sexy. I missed my husband and hoped we could move past this. I slid my middle finger between my legs and circled my clit at thoughts of it being his tongue. He was the pussy connoisseur. I circled my clit until my legs trembled and nut ran down the inside of my thighs. I was tired of playing with that rose shit and my fingers. I needed my husband.

By the time I finished my shower and dressed, I was back in the living room where MJ and the kids were sitting on the floor in a circle eating pizza and laughing. I grabbed my phone and took a picture to have this moment forever. It was like he fit perfectly with them, but not as a father. I didn't know the position but it was love for sure.

"Yo' ass was taking too long and they were hungry. Nah you gotta feed lil' man because his food come from yo' titties, and I ain't got that." He laughed and handed Mhayce to me. I sat on the sofa and breast fed him until he went to sleep. I missed this part about being a mother. Little things like rubbing his head and kissing his cheeks brought me great joy. Looking at Mhayce reminded me of Mhyia, and I started to cry. I missed my baby girl too.

"Nah, ain't no tears in here tonight." I looked up and MJ was looking at me. "You forgave yourself, don't dwell on it." He bit into his pizza as I looked around at the kids, who were oblivious as to what was going on.

"You right, fix me a plate while I go lay him on the other sofa," I told him as I got up. I reached to get my shorts out my ass, and he laughed.

"You like tempting a nigga, but I will enjoy the view." I turned and laughed at him as I put Mhayce down and surrounded him with pillows.

After filling my belly, we were in the living room chilling. The twins had their iPads occupying them as they lay in the middle of the room. Zheno had his iPad mini on his lap with his body tucked under MJ as he played the game. The scene was serene and peaceful. I'd dragged the basinet into the living room and put Mhayce in there so he could be more comfortable and wouldn't roll and fall off the sofa. Since everybody was okay, I decided to have me a drink of wine. I'd pumped all the milk I could and had back-up formula in case I ran out. I poured my glass and connected my phone to my Beats speaker. I was in a mood because I missed my husband, so I played the first Mary J. Blige song I could think of. Her music always spoke to my soul. The world knew when Mary was going through something because she told it through her music. When she was happy, her music was happy, but when that bitch was going through it, you went through it with her.

I'm not in love
It's just some kind of thing I'm goin' through
Goin' through, goin' through
And it's not infatuation
Ain't nothin' goin' on between me and you
Me and you, me and you
But I dream about it every night, baby
Wantin' you here with me
Makin' love to me
And oh
I'm missin' you like crazy
Body and soul is achin'
I'm out of control
Missing you so

I sang along with Mary J. because those words expressed just what I was going through. I sipped my wine and sang the song like my life depended on it. My emotions were all over the place as I thought about Mahsyn touching that bitch the way he touched me, loving that bitch the way he used to love on me. My thoughts were going to drive me insane.

God knows I'm tryin' to keep you out of my head
I ain't tryin' to love no one
I ain't tryin' to get hurt again, no
But there's something that just guts in my skin

And all I know is I can't let go
And that's the way it is
I'm missin you like crazy
Body and soul is achin'
I'm out of control
Missing you so

By the time the song ended, I was a ball of tears and the entire bottle was gone. I cried angry tears for my marriage, for my husband, and tears for that bitch because when I found out where the fuck she lived, those tears would be reversed and her family would be crying. I had been calling Jhewelz's dirty, sheisty ass because she had to know that my husband was fucking with her bestie. I had some hands for that bitch too. Maybe it wasn't meant for me and Mahsyn to be together. Our relationship happened so fast that we couldn't slow it down. I didn't because he saved me from a lot of shit. Maybe we didn't take the time to know each other long enough, but love didn't have a time on it. His possessiveness was what held me captive along with his protective nature.

"You good in here?" I heard MJ behind me. I tried to hurry and wipe my tears, but he was too close to me not to see them falling.

"If that nigga ain't here to choose you, then he don't deserve you, Nobby." He turned me to face him and hugged me tight.

"Nigga, who the fuck are you to tell my wife what the fuck she needs?" The hairs on my neck went wild as I turned, and Magnolia was standing in the door with death in his eyes.

MAGNOLIA

"**W**ho the fuck are you, nigga?!" I stepped further into the room where Chunky was hugging some young nigga with dreads. To see her even touching another nigga had me wanting to kill her and this nigga.

I knew it was fucked up to leave her at the court house, but that had to be done. Then, after the shit Mariah just dropped on me, I needed my wife. She was the only one who could stop my raging thoughts, to calm down the raging bull that lived inside of me, not Mahyesha. And I wasn't going to Dior because she had done enough damage. I needed my wife. My other half. I'd gotten her addy from Mahyesha. I didn't have her number, so I popped up. I eased through the front door because it wasn't locked. I noticed the girls and Zheno on the sofa, even Mhayce was in his lil' bed sleep. I heard the crying and music and followed the sound. I wouldn't have ever thought she would be in this bitch with a nigga that looked half her age. Dude let her go quick as fuck and backed away. Long as he didn't try to save her, he had his life. My problem wasn't with him but with her, because she was a married fucking woman. I knew I was using the double standard, because I fucked Dior, but as a woman she shouldn't have come back to my hood and fucked with a hood nigga.

"I know you not fucking playing with me, Zenobia. This nigga look 18! This what the fuck we doing now?!" I couldn't control my anger as I neared her.

"The fuck are you talking about, Magnolia?" Oh she was feeling herself, because she never called me that unless she was mad or we were fucking. Before I could control my hands, they were around her throat and I was dragging her to the nearest vacant room. If that nigga knew what was best for him, he would walk the fuck away now. I grabbed her neck, lifting her off her feet, and walked down the hallway with her trying to kick and scream, but she decided not to because it would disturb the kids. I went into the room and threw her on the bed.

"You got a nigga around my fucking kids, girl. Don't you know I will murder yo' ass? What the fuck is wrong with you? Watch yo' fucking words, because it's taking everything in me not to go upside yo' shit," I told her as she bounced up from the bed.

"Motherfucker, let's be clear, you put me the fuck out! I had no one to turn to and you knew that. I came back to where the fuck I belong. And you are right, he is young, but I'm not fucking him, unlike you, fucking a bitch that's trying to set you up," she yelled, getting in my face. Her eyes held tears that she wouldn't let fall because I taught her that shit.

"You showed me that you didn't give a fuck about me the day you dragged me out of our home like I was fucking trash," she shouted to my chest because she couldn't reach my face.

"You killed my fucking daughter! The fuck you expected me to do?!" I barked in her face, and she cowered. I knew that was a low blow, but seeing her with another nigga activated my next level of crazy. She froze. Her body went completely stiff. I couldn't take the words back. They left a bad taste in my mouth. She backed away from me, looking into my eyes. Her eyes turned to slits, face beet red, body shaking. I had fucked up, fumbled her heart.

"Now we can address the fucking elephant in the room!" she screamed, cracking her neck from left to right. I wanted to run because she looked like the devil was running through her body, and she transformed to another person right before my eyes.

"Yes, I murdered our fucking daughter, but I didn't mean to. I was overwhelmed. The thought of me raising a daughter like my mother raised me scared the fuck out of me. I live with the regret of hurting something our love created every day that I open my fucking eyes. I needed you, but the fucking streets needed you more. I was crying out for you to stay, be my husband, but whatever fucking beef you had was more important than your wife and family. If you think I'm fucking that young ass boy, then have at it. You been fucking a bitch that ain't me, right?" She walked closer to me, and I backed up. I learned from her being pregnant what her hands could do. I couldn't answer because she was right. I was fucking Dior, but it was only once.

"You let a bitch see a side of you that you didn't let me see, right? She a psychiatrist, right? But yet you said I was your fucking medicine? If I was your medicine, you should have fucking come to me and we healed together, not run and fall for the first bitch you talk to." She was hurt because with each word, tears fell down her eyes. I wanted to comfort her, love her, but she would be too mad to let me. The tension was too thick.

"You did past shit to me that I let slide, Magnolia, because of the love we had." She was speaking in past tense, so I knew where this shit was going but I wouldn't let it. "When I met you, you lied to me. You were fucking married, and I still fucked with you because I believed you. Then, you fucked a bitch and got mad when I fucked Fhendi, and killed them both. You a selfish ass nigga, but I loved you through all of that. Yes, I fucked up bad by killing Mariah, but I forgave myself and so has God. At this point, I don't give a fuck about you forgiving me because you have to walk around with the fucking guilt of not being there for me when I needed you to be." She pushed me, but I didn't move. Her last statement pissed me off, and I hemmed her up against the wall.

"Who the fuck you told about Fhendi?" I pushed my body into hers. The little bitty shorts that covered her thick ass made my dick hard. I hadn't been this close to her in so long, just her breathing had me ready to fuck her.

"The fuck are you talking about? I didn't tell nobody that shit, you made me kill that man, remember? You questioning my fucking loyalty now? Get the fuck off me, nigga." She pushed me and I let her. I backed away from her, rubbing my hands over my head.

Whap, whap

She smacked my right then left cheek. I wanted to choke her the fuck out, but I deserved that. I never had a reason to question her loyalty.

"That bitch got your head that far gone that you questioning me now?! The fuck is wrong with you, Mahsyn? I didn't ask for this shit. I didn't ask to be disrespected and hurt by you. I would never do anything to jeopardize your fucking freedom, you dumb motherfucker." She tried to hit me again but I caught her hand, pulling her to me.

"I'm sorry." I put my lips to her neck. "I'm so fucking sorry, Chunky, for everything," I cried into her neck as I kissed it.

"No, get the fuck off me." She put up a fight but not enough for me to back away. I needed her and I was about to show her.

"I love you, Chunky, my mind just fucked up. I know you didn't mean to kill our daughter, but this shit hurts, man. I feel like I'm disrespecting her if I forgive you," I told her honestly, and she backed away from me.

"Then get the fuck out!" She yanked away from me, only for me to pull her back to me. "Go play with your doctor bitch where you ain't gotta worry about forgiveness, because you don't know that hoe like you think you do." This time I backed away because she pissed me off.

"Since you know so much, do you know that Fhendi was her fucking husband? That nigga was lying to yo' fucking face, and you fell for it. Dior thinks that her husband will one day come back fucking home and love her again, but he not because we fucking killed him. This woman opened her heart to me about her husband that we fucking killed, and she don't even know. She don't fucking know she was talking to the nigga that killed her husband. Her fucking father said there is a CI that could put me away forever. What the fuck do you think I was in jail for, Zenobia?" I told her, and she walked up to me.

"You really think I'll let them white boyz take you from yo' fucking kids?" She cocked her head to the side. I was confused, but I didn't ask questions.

"I know you wouldn't." I smirked at her because her ass was crazy just like me.

I walked to her, lifting her ass all the way to the ceiling. I was pissed because she had another nigga looking at my shit. She wrapped her thighs around my neck. I used my teeth to pull her shorts to the side, and she didn't have on panties. Her essence smelled like vanilla and her. Her pussy was golden, and I'd never get enough of it. She moved her hips, throwing her pussy lips against my face.

"Eat this pussy, Magnolia." I looked up at her and licked my lips, and I tongue kissed her clit. Her hands rubbed through my waves as her juices wet up my beard. Her pussy was just the way I left it, tight and untouched, because she knew better. I slurped her clit as my tongue found her hole and eased in.

"Oh my god!" she screamed, and I tapped her thighs for her to pipe down because she had company downstairs.

"You want that nigga to hear how I'm eating your pussy?" I asked, mouth full of pussy.

"I don't give a fuck what that nigga hear," she moaned loud as fuck. I gripped her hips while flattening my tongue, applying pressure to her clit.

"Mmmmm," I moaned in her shit because she tasted so

fucking good. Her clit engorged twice before her nut gushed in my mouth, and I drank that shit like a big glass of milk. I walked over to the wall, easing her down to wrap her legs around my waist. She held on for dear life as I fumbled with my pants to set my dick free.

I grabbed her hands and put them above her head. She moved against me until my tip found her opening, and started to grind on it. He was riding the head because I wouldn't push all the way in. Her pussy was dripping for me. I felt the heat from her pussy, and it made my knees buckle.

"Stop teasing me and give me that dick, Magnolia." She sucked my top then bottom lip. I was always weak for her kisses, weak for her period.

I lined my dick up with her wet opening and pushed all the way in, touching her soul. Her shit was warm and so fucking tight. I held inside her because my shit started thumping. She tried to move, but I intertwined our hands and gripped her hands tighter.

"Don't fucking move, Chunky," I whispered in her ear, and she laughed.

"That dick thumping for me, huh? I can feel how much he misses me, fuck." She gripped her muscles around my dick, and I had to start moving.

"Fuck, Chunky," I moaned with her titty in my mouth. I bit down on her nipple, and her walls gripped me tighter. I backed up until we were on the bed with her on top. I grabbed her hips as she planted both her feet on the bed and started bouncing up and down.

"Slow the fuck down," I growled, because I was trying to hold my nut, but she was killing me. Her dreads fell over on top of my stomach. The sight was burning my eyes as she fucked me like she missed me. I had to take control of the situation. I picked her up, lifting us both from the bed, and turned her around. I threw her against the dresser and slid back in. Her shit felt tighter and warmer than a George Foreman grill. I grabbed the back of her dreads to control the stroke, but she threw all that ass back on a nigga, and I knew I should have let her ride this dick.

"I miss this dick, Magnolia. How could you keep it from me?" She looked back at me like she was possessed by the fucking devil. I really turned her the fuck out.

"I'on know, but on God, I'll never keep it from you again," I moaned, and I leaned over and kissed up her spine. That slowed her ass down. I kissed up to her neck until I got to her ear.

"I forgive you, Chunky, but just give a nigga some time, and get rid of that nigga that's around my kids." I went in deeper, damn near lifting her up off the floor.

"I don't need time, Magnolia, I need you." Her hand snaked behind her to grab my head, bringing me closer to her. This was devil sex. The sex that made fucking babies. Body to body, her back arched to my front, I dumped all my seeds inside of her womb. I knew I'd gotten her pregnant.

"I need you too," I told her as my hand caressed her clit. I felt her squirt in the palm of my hand. I brought my hand to my mouth and drunk that shit like it was water.

Chunky looked delirious. She was falling asleep standing up. I picked her up and carried her to the bed to lay her down. I went to the bathroom for a warm, soapy towel to clean her up. I walked back in the room and she was slightly snoring. I missed that sound. I missed the chokehold she used to have me in while we slept together. She would always say that she held me tight at night because she was scared I would disappear. After wiping her down, I put the cover over her and pulled my pants back around my waist. I stepped back into my shoes and tried to leave, but her voice stopped me.

"I knew you wouldn't stay, and it's cool." Her voice held sleep in it. "But tell MJ I'll be down there in a few hours to get the kids. Mhayce's breast milk is in the refrigerator because he might be hungry." She turned away from me and started snoring again.

My ears had to be fucking with me. Chunky had no idea that my fucking son was in her living room actually taking care of his siblings. Chunky could be so naive at times and so trusting, and I hated that shit. That was part of my story that I failed to tell Zenobia about because I wasn't proud of it, but I knew sooner or later what I had done in the dark would come to the light. I could have woken her up to tell her a secret that I'd been holding for a long time, but now wasn't the time. She needed to enjoy her afterglow. I was still fucked up myself about Mariah popping up out the blue. I needed to talk to this lil' nigga soon, but not now.

I walked into the living room. The twins were on one sofa asleep, Zheno was laid out across MJ's chest, and Mhayce's fat ass was on his shoulder. I stood there and watched for a minute. MJ was nothing like Mariah described him to be. A fucking menace because of the way he moved throughout the streets. I was reckless like that at one point. She forgot how the fuck I got down, and that's why I didn't want to bring a baby into this world back then. I walked over to the sofa and stood before him holding my sons. He looked at me like he saw Casper. He tried to move the kids, but I stopped him.

"Nah, you ain't gotta get up, I'm 'bout to head out. Thanks for looking out for my wife, son," I told him and saluted him. I looked into eyes that mirrored mine. I wanted so bad to tell him who I was, that he was babysitting his siblings and his bonus mother was upstairs asleep, but my mouth couldn't form the words.

"It's more like she looking out for me. She actually saving me from doing stupid shit. I know all about you from what she tells me. She really is sorry for what happened, and she loves the fuck outta you. I hope whatever y'all going through that y'all get through it, because they don't make them like her nomo," he told me, and that was straight facts.

"Don't I know it. She said his milk is in the fridge," I started to say, but he stopped me.

"I fed him already," he finished my statement, and I smirked.

"Have you and my wife ever—" I started again, and he cut me off.

"Nah, it don't matter how short her shorts are and how her ass hang out of them, I would never fuck with it like that. She sparing me for real on top of sparing other niggas' lives. Me being here is for my benefit more than it is hers," he told me, never breaking eye contact. I guess Chunky just had that effect on people.

"I trust you, lil' nigga, and I also trust that you know who the fuck I am and what that woman up there means to me." I nodded my head toward her room. "So you know what would happen if you fuck with that," I told him, and he nodded his head up and down.

"You got my word, chief, and I stand on that, all ten." I saluted him and left out the door with a heavy heart. That was the first conversation I'd had with my fucking son.

❦ 13 ❦

DIOR

I'm too young to be this rich (Rich)
We can shoot it out or just beat a bitch (Woo, woo)
They say I'm gettin' thick, "What you eatin' sis'?" (Thick)
I been on my bully like a mean bitch (Ayy)
These bitches fraud, they cap a lot (Cap a lot)
Reach for this chain, I'ma slap you out
First person throw some shit at me on stage
We beatin' they ass in the parkin' lot (Woo, woo, woo)
I smell like money and Baccarat (Ooh)
Fendi space boots, like an astronaut (Ooh)
I swear if I said it, I meant it, I handlin' business
Ain't rappin' on shit that I'm not about
Don't ask 'bout a nigga I forgot about
Boss bitches only, you is not allowed, cut it out
Self-made bitch, hell you talking 'bout?
Yeah I got it out the mud, no handout (Bitch)

I looked good and felt even better as Latto's "He Say, She Say" bumped at a high volume through the speakers as she described how I was feeling. I hadn't talked to Mahsyn in weeks, and I was fine with that. It was time to move on. I was mad at Jhewelz because even after she realized who Mahsyn and Zenobia were, she still was team Zenobia. I even explained to her how my father tried to frame Mahsyn for my husband's death. She then told me that I really didn't know who the fuck Mahsyn was, and I told that I didn't care because I wanted to be with him. There was no way he would take his wife back after what she did. I knew he would make his way back to me because this shit couldn't happen to me twice. I knew Fhendi was dead. I knew a lot of shit that people thought I didn't know.

It was time to get back to business, though. My office had been closed for three weeks and my appointments were through the roof. Pulling up to my establishment, I felt accomplished. I was a black woman who owned her own practice. I built my shit from the ground up with the help of Fhendi's drug money. Let's be clear, I knew what the fuck Fhendi did for a living. I let him push his illegal money through my practice. Why he disappeared? He didn't disappear, and I knew that Magnolia killed him. I couldn't let my father put him away, but I had bigger plans for his ass.

I parked in my designated parking space and grabbed my phone and Birkin bag. I strutted inside my building, bypassed my receptionist, and went to my office. I sat down in my chair and buzzed for my assistant to come in.

"Good morning, Dr. Maverick, what can I get you?" She stuck her head in the door.

"Run to Starbucks and grab me a mocha crunch and a brownie, please," I told her, and she nodded her head and left out. I felt like eating sweets today. It'd been like that for the past week, but I ignored it because I would get back in the gym to work it off. I knew I had gained weight because all I did while I was off was eat and sleep. No contact with the outside world unless I ordered food.

Forty-five minutes had passed and my assistant still hadn't brought my shit back, and my stomach was growling. Starbucks was walking distance, so what the fuck was taking her so long? I was hungry. If I knew she would take so damn long, I would have went and gotten it myself. I grabbed my purse and was about to get up when the door opened.

"You going somewhere?" I looked up as Mahsyn swagged into my office holding my drink and brownie, looking like a tall glass of mocha milk. That was only way I could describe his skin color. He was a light-skin man, but the rays of his skin had mocha specks in it.

He walked in, closing the door behind him and sitting my stuff on the desk. I wanted to jump in his arms, but a part of me told me this wasn't a social call. I felt like he was about to fuck with my feelings.

"I remember when I first walked in here demanding a refill on my medication, and you refused to give it to me." He walked around to the back of my desk, pushing my chair back. He sat down on my desk and looked at me.

"You look different. Is there something you wanna tell me?" The way he said that had my soul shaking. Like he knew what I was up to. I smiled as I tried to get up. I pushed my hair behind my ear and tried to stand, but he slightly pushed me back in my seat.

"Why are you acting nervous when I came all this way here to see you?" A smiled graced his lips but didn't meet his eyes. The sinister gloss in his beautiful eyes didn't go unnoticed. I sat back down with my hands in my lap. He reached around my desk and got my drink and handed it to me.

"Drink." He stared at me as I put my straw in my drink and took a sip. I hoped he didn't poison this shit and was trying to kill me. He stared a little too hard at me while I was drinking, but this bitch was good. I swallowed it up and was ready for my brownie, but he wouldn't give it to me.

"You was hungry, huh?" He looked me up and down with lust. I crossed my legs to stop my clit from jumping, because I was on full attack mode. I wanted that dick in the worst way, but I had to feel him out a little first. Our last encounter wasn't a good one. I wasn't about to go with my move only to be shot down.

"Yeah, my appetite picked up lately but for sweets." I smiled, hoping to break his icy stare.

"That's because you are sweet." He pulled me from the chair and against his body. I melted when his huge arms circled my waist, pulling me into his hard body. His head went to my neck as his tongue formed circles until he sucked the same spot. My pussy walls clenched as he palmed my ass. I moaned as he reached between us and pulled my skirt up.

"I know she misses me." He slid my panties to the side and slid his middle finger inside my walls. My hands left the back of his head and grabbed his shoulders as my head fell into his chest.

"Mahsyn," I moaned his name and felt his dick spring to life. My mouth watered. I had to taste him.

I backed away from him, causing his hand to slip from under my skirt. I pulled at his joggers until they were to his ankles and pushed him to sit in the chair.

"Damn, it's like that?" I heard him suck in air as he fell back in the seat. I squatted in front of him. I sucked his golden tip while my hands massaged his shaft and balls.

"You gon' put a mouth on it or just play with it?" he moaned, looking down at me. I swallowed him whole, letting his dick go past my tonsils. I slurped and suctioned my jaws, gripping his dick like my pussy would. Watching the look in his eyes made my pussy leak. My head bobbed up and down, and I felt his ass cheeks tighten. I made sure to make it extra sloppy for him because I knew he would love it, what nigga didn't? I felt his hand go the back of my head, guiding my movements to satisfy him. I left his shaft alone and sucked on his balls, and he sucked in air. My hands massaged his shaft while my tongue took care of his balls.

"You trying to kill a nigga." I felt his dick thumping. He was about to nut. He yanked me up by my hair and slammed my body down on his dick. His strokes were fast but deadly. I bounced up and down wildly as he held on for the ride. This wasn't love making. This was raw fucking. He grabbed my legs in the crook of each arm and stood from the chair. He stood in that position and fucked the lining out my pussy, and I enjoyed every minute of it. He pushed the paperwork off my desk, putting my ass on the end of it, and fucked me until his seeds were left inside of me. No kissing and barely any foreplay. That shit made me feel some type of way. He was fucking me like a whore, and I didn't like it. After he got his fucking rocks off, he let my legs down and pulled up his joggers and went back to the other side of my desk like nothing happened.

"Are you fucking serious, Mahsyn?" I pulled my clothes down and sat down. I would clean myself later.

"I got my nut and you got yours. I ain't ask you to suck my dick, that was your doing," he told me nonchalantly, like I wasn't shit. I felt played, like a side bitch.

"Do you fuck yo' wife like that?" I didn't mean for that to come out, but I said what the fuck I said.

"It depends on the day of the week and if she feel like role playing, but that ain't got fuck to do with you, and it sure in the fuck don't concern you," he told me in a tone that I'd never heard before.

"This must be the infamous Magnolia that everybody speaks so highly of that's finally showing his face." I crossed my arms under my breasts and narrowed my eyes at him.

"If you would have given me my fucking medicine like I asked months ago, we wouldn't be at this fucking point, and yo'

father wouldn't be trying to put a nigga under the fucking jail."
He raised his voice, but that shit didn't move me. I pulled out
my prescription pad to write his meds out. I ripped the paper off
and slid it across the desk to him.

"You happy now?" I asked him, rolling my eyes.

"Not really, but I need some information from you. How the
fuck did yo' pops get pictures of my entire family?" he asked me,
and I didn't know. I didn't have the answer to that because Jason
didn't tell me anything about work. I hadn't talked to him since
the shit happened.

"What pictures are you talking about?" I asked him. He
sprung to his feet and was in my face with his hand around my
neck.

"The fucking pictures of my entire family, including my dead
fucking daughter. The only person that knew about the shit
outside my family was yo' ass. Bitch, you better find me some
answers, or yo' paw gon' be trying to find your fucking body." He
pushed me in the chair, and the tears pooled in my eyes. I
couldn't believe this was the same man that catered to my every
need at my house.

"And as far as Magnolia surfacing, you ain't seen a fucking
thing yet. I'm not the nigga to fuck with when yo' people trying
to fuck with my freedom. You gon' find out who the fuck
running their mouth or you gotta suck yo' paw dick, bitch." My
heart was crushing with every word he spat at me.

"How can you say that when I'm carrying yo' baby, Mahsyn?"
He looked at me like I'd spit on his shoes.

"You pregnant, bitch?" He looked at me like he wanted to
kill me.

"My name is Dr. Dior and yes, I am." He looked at me before
walking out my door, shattering the glass from slamming it so
hard. I put my head on the desk and cried until I heard my door
creak open.

"Pick up yo' fucking face. I told you that nigga wasn't one to be fucked with, and I hope you learned your lesson." That was Jhewelz coming around my desk to console me. I may be crying now, but with the plan I had in motion for him, jail wasn't the only fucking thing he had to worry about.

❧ 14 ❧
MJ

"**D**amn, Lexi, throw that pussy back on a nigga." I smacked her ass as her thick thighs smacked against mine. I needed some type of release, and Lexi was the perfect bitch to do it. She was the same bitch who I was talking to the day Nobby called herself being messy and petty.

After the situation with Magnolia, I had an entire new outlook on life. I knew he loved Nobby, and I hoped they got their shit together. Lexi was throwing this pussy on a nigga, had me wanting to take a condom off and hit the pussy raw, but I didn't want her to get the wrong impression. Women thought when a nigga hit the pussy raw that we become one, but that wasn't the case. The only thing I chased was money. Nothing came before that but time with Nobby and the kids.

The past few weeks I had been in and out of Nobby's house, but I had to make this money. I didn't want to leave because I felt like I belonged when I was at her house, but money had to be made and my men had bills to pay. Some nigga named Endymion and his crew was trying to put me down on the streets, but I wasn't letting up. It was foot to neck season, and it was my time. Them old niggas needed to step to the side and let a young nigga ride.

I'd done my research on Magnolia and the Masons, and that nigga was caked. That's how I was trying to be when I retired out the game, but I was just getting started, so there was no stopping me now. He retired with a clean record and got the fuck out of New Orleans. I was trying to be like that nigga. I had a port in Miami that was my plug, and that nigga's crew couldn't handle it. He didn't want to pass the crown to me, so I was ready to dethrone him.

"Oh, fuck." I felt my nut rising to the tip of my dick, and Lexi's nasty ass stopped and turned to me, pulling the condom off, and let me nut all in her face. She beat my shit until my nuts were empty. I fell back on the bed exhausted. I watched as she switched her thick ass to the bathroom to get a soapy towel to clean a nigga's dick. I closed my eyes for a second before my phone rang. Thinking it was Nobby, because I hadn't talked to her in few days, I grabbed it without looking at the screen.

"What's up, Nobby?" I answered, because I just knew it was her.

"Who the hell is Nobby, Mahsyn Jr.?" It was my mother's voice, and I jumped out the bed as Lexi wiped my dick off. I put on my boxers and jeans and threw my shirt over my head.

"That's my friend, Ma. What's up, Ma, you in the city?" I asked her, because that's the only time she called me.

"Yeah, son, I hear you been calm in the streets. Yes, I am in the city and wanted to meet with you. I need to talk to you about something." Her voice was serious. I hoped she wasn't about to meet me to talk about me moving to New York, because it wasn't happening.

"Drop the location and I'll meet you there in 30 minutes," I told her and finished getting dressed. I left Lexi's apartment while she was in the shower because I didn't feel like explaining to her while I wasn't spending the day with her. I left her a nice knot of money on her dresser and slid out the door to my truck. I connected my phone to the car to call Nobby.

"Well, look who decided to check on me after days of getting some pussy. What you want, MJ?" Nobby answered the phone, laughing.

"I had to get some type of release but look, I was calling you to tell you that my mother wanted to meet me. You think I should go?" I asked her like I needed her permission. It's crazy the type of friendship we had.

"She's your mother, boy, go be civil and see what she wants," she told me, and I agreed.

"Okay, what you got up for today?" I asked her, changing the subject.

"Nothing, I'm on break from school so me and the kids gon' chill today. I might have to sign up for online classes if the kids stay here with me," she said, and I could feel the hurt in her voice. She hadn't talked to Magnolia since the night he came there and fucked her into a coma

"Don't worry, that nigga coming back," I told her, and I meant it. I saw the love in his eyes. He just had some shit to handle.

"Don't worry about me. Go meet your mother and come this way when you done, because I wanna hear every detail," she told me, and we disconnected the call.

I checked my phone and saw that she wanted me to meet her at Starbucks on Claiborne. It was cool with me, but I would have much rather meet somewhere we could eat, because I didn't like coffee. It took me 20 minutes to get there. I took a big breath to prepare myself for whatever she had to say. I got out my car and went inside, and her beautiful face was the first face I saw. I loved my mother, but I didn't like the fact that she tried to run my life. I graduated from high school, but she wanted me to follow in her footsteps and go to pharmacy school, but I was a street pharmacist. College wasn't in the stars for me, or at least it wasn't at the moment. I slid in the seat across from her and she smiled. I reached over to kiss her cheek. My mother was beautiful. Fair skin, beautiful hair, slanted gray eyes that I inherited.

"What's up, Ma, what's wrong?" I saw the sadness in her eyes, and I knew something was up. She didn't agree with the shit I did for a living, but I would shut the fucking city down behind Mariah. She put her head down but her eyes quickly met mine.

"I didn't call you down here to fuck up your day or your life for that matter, but I need to discuss some things with you." She reached across the table for my hands, and her eyes watered. I didn't like where this shit was going.

"I know you been keeping company with Zenobia. I know her from high school," she said, and I was confused. My mother was older than Nobby.

"I am older than her, but we went to the same high school. I know you been spending a lot of time with her and her kids. I appreciate her for keeping you safe and out the streets. She was saving you, son." I knew she was, and I would forever respect her for that.

"Don't look at me like that. I always know what's going on when it comes to you, MJ," she said and continued, "Baby, I need you to not be upset and your temper take you out of character when I tell you this." Her grip on my hands grew tighter, and my heart started to beat rapidly. Whatever she was about to tell me would probably change my life forever.

"Remember when we discussed your father and the situation we were in when I got pregnant with you?" she asked me, and I nodded my head. I remember the story but put it to the back of my mind because my father didn't know about me.

"Well, I reached out to him a few weeks back and told him about you. I just didn't want you to walk around thinking he didn't know about you, because he does."

"Okay, well who is he, Ma? And stop stalling," I told her as my legs shook underneath the table.

"Magnolia is your daddy, son." I had to be fucking tripping, because I know she didn't just say that shit.

"What the fuck did you just say?" Respect went out the window, because she betrayed me. I looked this nigga in his eyes, and he didn't say shit. I had his kids, my fucking siblings, hanging all over me and didn't even know it. I was livid yet crushed, because I didn't expect this type of shit from my mother. I pulled my hands away from hers and stood to my feet. The fire in me couldn't calm as I flipped the fucking table over, knocking shit everywhere. I didn't give a fuck if we got put out this shit. You just don't drop some shit like this on me like that.

"Did Zenobia fucking know?" I gritted my teeth as I thought about the way she fucked with me hard. She cared about me like I was her fucking brother.

"No, she didn't, because Magnolia never told her." That made me even more mad, because this nigga felt like he could hide me from the world.

"It's not his fault. I kept him from knowing about you, Mahsyn Jr." I turned around and looked at her.

"You have me that nigga name too?" I asked, bewildered. I hated my name. The was the sole reason I never told it to Nobby, the irony.

"You were his first-born son, and he was my first love. I needed a piece of him with me," she said as she stood from the table and put her oversized shades on.

"I hope that one day you can find it in your heart to forgive me, because I am sorry." She kissed my cheek and left out the coffee shop, never looking back.

I didn't ask for a fucking chapter in this book, and I for damn sure didn't ask to be Magnolia's fucking son, but as always, Miss Jazzie brings a fucking plot twist. I can't believe she made me this nigga son and my mommy sheisty as fuck. That's why Nobby never looked at me like that, even though she was sexy as fuck. That further explained why Magnolia didn't kill me for hugging his wife. That was now my fucking bonus mother. How the fuck was I going to explain this shit to her without Magnolia being put in the doghouse? Because this nigga fell off the grid. I didn't wanna tell her before he got a chance to, but what the fuck was I supposed to tell her when I got to her house and her messy ass wanted all the tea? I didn't want to lie to her. I needed to get in touch with Magnolia for a man-to-man sit down, because I would rather the shit come from his mouth than mine. I walked to my car with some heavy shit on my mind, but I knew I couldn't avoid Nobby because she would call my phone and pop up at all my spots until I answered her. I headed to her house, hoping that my face didn't show what the fuck I was feeling.

❦ 15 ❦

MAGNOLIA

I knew this bitch wasn't pregnant. She couldn't be. We only fucked twice, and I know what y'all thinking. I know it only takes once, so she must've gotten pregnant the first time we fucked at her house. This was not a part of the fucking plan. I was supposed to go to her, fuck her for info, and dip out, but all that changed when she dropped the pregnancy bomb on a nigga. I wanted to kill that bitch in her office, but that would have left too many witnesses. I had to play this shit smart or I was going to lose my fucking wife. Thinking about her, I needed to know how the fuck she got the twins. I was supposed to ask her, but the pussy got in the way and had a nigga mind gone, per usual. I needed to talk to someone, and I called the only person who would understand.

"You and my daughter made up yet? Y'all must've did, because she still got the kids and I'm in Atlanta with my husband, so what yo' ass want?" Mahyesha didn't have no filter.

"Ma, I fucked up. I got a fucking son out here that I knew nothing about. What the fuck am I supposed to tell Nobby?" I asked her, and she took a deep breath.

"The fucking truth. You didn't know about the boy, Mahsyn, but I did. When I saw Nobby with that young man, I knew he

79

was your son. I just hoped that she wasn't fucking him, because that would have been some nasty shit." She laughed, but I was serious. "Stop overthinking shit. Nobby loves you. Fuck, at least she already got a relationship with her bonus son." I had to laugh at that, because Chunky really didn't know she was saving my son's life.

"Dior is pregnant." I slipped that in, and her laughing stopped.

"The fuck you mean she pregnant?! You didn't strap yo' dick up fucking with her? What the fuck is wrong with you, Mahsyn?" she asked me, and I knew she was angry because she didn't raise me like that.

"You have a fucking wife begging for your forgiveness, and this is what you bringing to the table?" she asked me, and I didn't have an answer. I didn't know what the fuck I was gonna do.

"Don't get quiet now. You know what the fuck you gotta do, you ain't new to this shit. When we have a threat to the family, how do we handle it?" she asked me, and I grinned.

"We dead it," I told her, and she agreed and ended the call.

My next call was to Endymion, because I needed him to call off his fucking dogs, because this was my son we were talking about fucking the streets up.

"Niggaaaa," he answered on the first ring. His voice told me he had some shit to tell me.

"What's up?" I would let him go first because my shit wouldn't take that long.

"Yo' wife is fucking evil, my nigga. You gotta get control of her and quick before she fuck some shit up." I pulled the phone away from my ear, confused. What the fuck had Chunky done that I didn't know about?

"The fuck you talking 'bout, nigga? Speak." I was heated.

"Man, a few weeks back, Zenobia came to Khency about some shit about hearing Candyce in the mall talking to somebody about setting you up with the feds. Zenobia was in the mall getting yo' shit for court when she ran across the bitch. One of the twins saw her but didn't say shit. Next thing I know, Khency telling me that Zenobia wanted Candyce canceled so she could get the girls because she missed them. Fuck, I thought Candyce was dead," he said all in one breath, and my mind was even more fucked up than before. Zenobia was getting more and more crazy as the days went by. "I got some of my hittas to drag that bitch out her apartment in Baton Rouge and bring her to the Dragon's Den. The bitch been there ever since. I don't even know if she still alive but per Zenobia, she wanted to wait for your call for the kill shot because this bitch was the op," he said, and I couldn't believe it. Even when I hated Chunky, she still came through for a nigga. I smiled on the inside, but her doing that shit made my blood boil.

"What the fuck you trying to do, nigga? You know we don't hold shit too long because it'll start stinking," he spoke in code.

"Hit the kill switch," I told him.

"Say less, but what you wanted to run some shit with me?" he asked me, and just that fast, I had forgotten the reason I called his ass. My world was falling apart and there was nothing I could do to stop it.

"The lil' nigga that's fucking with the work, that's my son. That shit just dropped in my lap. I need your hittas to stand down or I will step in." I made myself very clear about what the fuck I was saying. I ran the streets in New Orleans. I wouldn't hesitate to make KOE step down. I wasn't throwing my weight around, but I needed this nigga to know how serious I was about fucking with my seed.

"You good, bro, that lil' nigga and his crew ain't been making no noise anyway. I been called my hittas off them," he said. "Good luck with the shit I just told you, and I hope y'all work shit out and be together." Him saying that made me think about Chunky and the fact that Dior was pregnant. I couldn't go home until I tied up all my loose ends, and that started with talking to Chunky about my son.

"I will, nigga, thanks for that," I told him and hung the

phone up. Before I could throw my phone on the seat, it rang again, Jahari.

"What, bruh?" I didn't even have the energy to laugh with his messy ass.

"Nigga, I can't leave you by yourself without you getting into some shit. What the fuck is going on with you?" he asked, laughing.

"Nigga, don't act like Momma didn't call and tell you everything that I just told her, because I know her messy ass did."

"I sure in the fuck did." Her voice came booming through the speaker. This nigga had called me on 3-way.

"That was some loyal shit that Zee did, bruh. You gotta give her flowers for that after what the fuck you did to her. Amerika would have slaughtered my ass to death." I had to laugh, because she would have. "Yo' ass lucky we got Zyrese, or we would have been on the next flight out to whip yo' ass for getting that bitch pregnant," he said, and I laughed harder because he knew he couldn't fuck with these hands.

"So Candyce was the CI, huh?" Jahari asked me, and I didn't answer. I didn't like to talk over fucking phones, but he got the hint.

"Sounds like sis handling business down there but you fuckin up on yo' end." He had to throw that shit in there. "You need me for anything?" he asked sincerely.

"Nah, I know what I gotta do, and I'll get it done," I told them, and we said our I love you's before disconnecting the call. I had to get ahold of my life before I lost it all.

❧ 16 ❧
ZENOBIA

"**W**here the fuck you going dressed like a fucking ninja with that plastic ass jump suit on? You 'bout to play *Mortal Kombat?*" I hated MJ and his fucking jokes, but I needed him right now. I needed him to take care of the kids while I went to handle some shit.

Khency called me earlier telling me that Endymion talked to Mahsyn and he gave word for the kill shot, but he wanted to be the one to do it. This nigga had me fucked up. I did the foot work, so I was definitely gon' finish what I started. He had to beat me there to get her first.

"First of all, bastard, it's not plastic, it's leather, and come zip my shit up," I told him as he watched me get dressed.

"And don't think I believe that shit about yo' momma not showing up. Something happened because you been acting all depressed and weird since the shit happened, so you lying about something, but it's cool." I pulled my locs to the side so he could zip me up.

"That shit tight as fuck. Can you breath?" He was trying to be funny.

"Don't be funny, stupid ass," I told him and went to my bed. I lifted the mattress, and there was an array of guns, but for this all I needed was my 45.

"Yo, where the fuck did you get all that shit from?" His eyes got big as fuck.

"Stop being so fucking nosey, and you must've forgot who my husband is. He always taught me how to protect myself even when he wasn't around." I noticed his face change, but I ignored it. I tucked the gun in my holster and grabbed my mini jacket to conceal it.

"I'm going to handle grown-up business and I need you here if the kids wake up," I told him.

"I wanna see what yo' ass gotta do. I'm grown too," he told me, and I laughed. MJ was so protective over me that if I broke a nail he would kill who broke it.

"I got this one, MJ, so chill." I slid into my combat boots and left out the room with him on my heels.

"I'll call you if I need assistance, but I won't be gone long," I told him, and he kissed my cheek before I left out the door and jumped in my car.

I made it to the Dragon's Den in 20 minutes and went in through the back. Endymion was waiting by the door and escorted me to where Candyce was being held.

"Sis, you might wanna hurry up before Magnolia get here and beat you to it," he said, and I laughed.

"Dymi, that nigga in Atlanta scared out his fucking mind to come home because he thinks I don't know that the doctor bitch is pregnant, but I know and I don't give a fuck. I'm handling my business by keeping his freedom, but he gotta hold his end of the bargain up. When he brings his ass back to me, that bitch and that baby better be fucking dead, or I'll do it." I looked in his eyes so he could know I was serious. Mahyesha's messy ass had already called me and told me what happened, but I still felt like she wasn't telling me everything, but I took what I could get. She said it was some shit Magnolia had to discuss with me that she wouldn't, so I was cool with it. Whatever else he had to say, we would get through.

"Damn, I guess nothing gets past yo' ass, huh?" He laughed and I did too.

"And don't," I told him as we walked in the room.

I felt vomit rise in my throat as the smell of piss and feces filled the room. Candyce sat strapped to a chair in the middle of the room with guards around her ready to shoot. Dymi handed me a mask because it was stank as fuck in there.

"I don't need y'all, but Dymi can stay." I looked around at the guards, but they didn't budge. Dymi nodded his head and they filed out one by one, leaving us with her. I walked closer to her. I pulled my mask down and spit in her face. He gave me gloves and a jacket to put on to avoid blood splatter.

"Bitch, you thought you were gonna take my husband away from me and my kids?" I cocked my head to the side and pulled my gun out. I aimed it to the middle of her forehead, waiting on her to answer.

"Bitch, you mean my fucking twins?" she said with blood spilling from her mouth. The girls I got to beat her ass did a number on her. Both her eyes were swollen shut. I was surprised that she could fucking see me. She had deep flesh wounds and bruises everywhere. Her feet were crooked to the side like they were broken. Bitch feet looked like the man's feet off *Misery*.

"Bitch, those my twins. They won't even know you existed. I'ma love all your nastiness out of them while you rot in hell." I pushed the gun deeper in her head.

Even when this bitch was about to meet her maker, she was talking shit.

"No face, no case, you snitch ass bitch." I let two off into her dome and watched as the smoke permeated the wounds. I turned to Dymi, handing him the gun.

"Put that bitch in the furnace, I gotta get back home to the kids," I told him as I removed my white doctor jacket and gloves, throwing it at her body. I walked away from him and out the back door to my car and headed home. When Mahsyn went back to court next month, there would be no CI and no fucking case to solve.

I pulled up in my parking spot and hopped on the elevator. My adrenaline was dwindling, and I realized I'd just killed somebody. I'd just killed Mahsyn's first wife, but I had good reason. This bitch had to know that I would find out that she was talking to the feds. The hood don't sleep. It didn't matter where you went, you couldn't hide, and she had to learn that the hard way. I felt no remorse for doing what had to be done, but I did have some words for Mahsyn. Why would he keep shit from me when we made a pact that we would never keep secrets because secrets got you killed. I stood on the elevator and cried a hard cry. I cried for my marriage. I cried because I had to look at the twins and raise them knowing I killed their mother. I was just a ball of emotions. I cleaned my face before getting off the elevator and going inside the door.

When I walked in, MJ had Zheno sitting on the countertop eating ravioli, and the twins were at the table eating the same. Mhayce was in his arms as he fed him a bottle. I looked at them and smiled. MJ looked me up and down and frowned. I walked closer in the room, but he put his arm out to stop me.

"You got blood on our shoes. Go take that shit off before you take him from me." That shit came out more like a demand, but I walked away from him and went to my room to shower.

After getting myself together, I walked back in the room, but all the kids were asleep. MJ was sitting on the sofa playing the game. I plopped next to him and grabbed the other controller and started to play *Grand Theft Auto* with him.

"What's up, nigga? You been acting weird," I asked him, but he didn't answer. He had been doing that for the past few days every time I asked him that. I grabbed the controller out his hand and pulled the entire game out, but I didn't give a fuck because I didn't like the quietness that surrounded us.

"The fuck, Nobby?!" he yelled, standing to his feet, and I stood with him.

"What the fuck is wrong with you? You come in here and play with the kids but when I try to talk to yo' ass, you brush me off. Did I do yo' ass something? Nah, that ain't it," I said, getting in his face. "Ya momma did meet you the other day, but what the fuck did she tell you that got you closed off with me?" I asked him, and he stared at me hard as fuck. Chill bumps ran across my skin. It looked so familiar that it scared me. He looked down at me before speaking.

"Since yo' ass so nosey, who the fuck did you go and kill?" he asked, and I met his stare.

"A bitch that was a threat to my family. Nah what the fuck is up with you?" I had no reason to lie to him because I would fuck a bitch up that was a threat to him. His shoulders slouched a little before he spoke again.

"My mother, Mariah, knows you. She said some shit about y'all going to school together, but she's older than you." I didn't know a bitch named Mariah, but I continued to listen. " She felt the need to tell me about my father and that he wanted to know me." I smiled and hugged him, but he pushed me away and went to grab his phone and keys and walked toward the front door.

"Wait, didn't you want to know who and where your father was? So why are you leaving, and why the fuck are you mad? I ain't ya damn daddy," I told him, because he was acting too weird. He pulled the door open and turned to me.

"The reason I never told you my real name was because I hated it, but when my mother told me who my father was, all this shit was starting to make sense. MJ stands for Mahsyn fucking Junior," he said before walking out the door, slamming it in my face.

MJ was Magnolia's son, but why was he mad with me? I didn't know shit about it. I couldn't even be mad with my husband because if my memory served me correctly, Mahsyn told Mariah to kill the baby per MJ. If that shit ain't karma at its best.

✸ 17 ✸

JADORE DIOR

I hated this pregnancy, but I wanted the nigga. I craved him. Every part of my body and senses heightened at the thought of him, but he didn't want me or this baby. The morning sickness damn near killed me though. Everything I ate came right back up. Even some smells made me vomit. Jhewelz had given me the strongest dose of Zofran, but even that didn't work. She told me that the first trimester was the hardest, and I believed her because I thought I was dying a slow death. I fumbled the ball again, and this time there was no coming back from it. Mahsyn wanted information that I couldn't give him, and I refused to give up the resources I did have. I couldn't let the unknown of this baby bother me, but it did shift the plans that I had to take Magnolia down for killing my husband.

I didn't know if it was the pregnancy or my real feelings, but when Fhendi's brother came at me saying that Magnolia killed my husband, I put my plan into action. Fedore, Fhendi's brother, got ahold of some info that Magnolia decapitated Fhendi and he and his wife got rid of his body. He talked to me and looked in my face those days as I poured my heart out to him about how hurt I was, knowing he was the one who killed him. That was earth shattering. My heart didn't want him to hurt like I did, but my mind felt like he deserved everything that came his way. That fact that I was pregnant by my husband's killer didn't help me at all. It's like I loved him because we created a miracle, but I wanted him killed the way he killed my husband. He took him from me and thought he was going to get his happily ever after and I would suffer. I wiped my tears and let Beyoncé sing to me while I fixed my dinner.

I love to see you walk into the room
Body shining, lightin' up the place
And when you talk, everybody stop
'Cause they know you know just what to say, and
The way that you protect your friends
Baby, I respect you for that
And when you grow, you take everyone you love along
I love that shit

Don't fly me away
Don't need to buy a diamond key
To unlock my heart
You shelter my soul
You're my fire when I'm cold
I want you to know

You had me at hello (Hello)
Hello (Hello)
Hello (Hello)
You had me at hello (Hello)
Hello (Hello)
Hello (Hello)

It was many years ago (Ago)
Baby, when you (When you)
Stole my cool (Stole my cool)
'Cause you had me at hello (My cool, hello)
Hello (Hello)
Hello (Hello, hello)

That was the first song Fhendi and I danced to after we were married. He was my everything, and now I had nothing. Magnolia wouldn't have shit when I was done with his ass either. Although my feelings had changed since finding out I was pregnant, the plan still had to go on. Fedore wouldn't stop until he avenged his brother's murder, starting with Magnolia. I regret the day I ever got into the bed with Fedore and decided to help him with this bullshit. Magnolia decided his fate the day he stumbled into my office.

Ding dong

I knew who that was without looking at the camera. I set the table before making my way to the door. I opened the door, and in walked Fedore and three other niggas dressed in all black. They all kissed my cheek and took their seats at the table. I served everyone's food. We ate in silence until Fedore spoke up.

"I know shit is fucked up, but that nigga caused too much bloodshed in my family. First Mhaci, my father, and now Fhendi. This nigga gotta go, like now." His Haitian accent was strong. I was scared to tell him that I didn't want to go through with the plan anymore now that I was pregnant, but that would infuriate him even more. Fedore always was an angry man, and the death of his family only intensified it. I gave him all the information on Magnolia and his family, and he was going to take them out one by one.

"I know what has to happen, but I need to tell you something first," I told him, and he stood from his seat, followed by his men.

"What's up, Jadore?" He was ready for whatever.

"I'm pregnant for Magnolia. It wasn't supposed to happen like that, but I couldn't control it. You wanted me to get inside his head, and in order for me to do that, I had to let him inside of mine," I told him as I stood from the table, backing away from it.

"You fucking what?!" he yelled and pulled his gun out, putting the silencer on it. It wasn't like anybody would hear it anyway.

"I fell in love with the nigga that killed my husband and got pregnant. This wasn't supposed to be like this," I said, but my words fell on deaf ears.

Pew pew pew pew pew pew pew

Came from every direction as they riddled my entire body with bullets. I felt the burning sensation rip though my skin then exit out the back. They emptied their clips in me, and all I could do was take it. I clutched my stomach, thinking about the baby I was carrying, and prayed that God had mercy on my soul. I couldn't get to my gun fast enough and even if I did, I was outnumbered. I cooked for these niggas and this was the thanks I got.

"What the fuck?" I heard before my body fell to the ground, and everything faded to black as I met my maker.

❦ 18 ❦

MAGNOLIA

Something wasn't right. I had been calling Dior's phone all day and she didn't answer. I went by her office and it was closed down. Not just business hours closed, but there was a for sale sign on it. I knew I had to kill her when Ghiani said that Fhendi's brother had come out of hiding and linked up with Dior to try and take me out. This shit was all a set up to get me away from my wife and kids, and I fell for it. There was no way I would let them take me, so they had better know what they were up against. I could have called my people, but this was my shit and I had to fix it. I hadn't slept or ate in three days trying to wrap my mind around all the shit that had dropped into my lap and how I would explain it to Chunky. She would for sure leave a nigga or at least try to, because I wouldn't let her. Ain't no fucking out of this marriage. Dior would just have to die along with her brother-in-law for thinking they could play with me.

I took that long ass ride out to her house and cut the lights when I got to her driveway. I noticed two other cars aside from hers. I reached on my backseat and grabbed my AR15 with the extended clip. I made sure to keep my automatic with me. I grabbed it and got out my car, careful not to slam my door because it was eerily quiet. I crept around the back of the house and her back door was locked. I remember there was a side door that she always kept open for her plants to breathe and took that route. I eased in the door, making sure my shit was cocked, and I searched every room on the first level. It was dark everywhere until I got to the living room area. The light was bright as fuck, but I paused when I heard niggas talking.

"How the fuck she gon' get pregnant by the nigga that killed her fucking husband and my entire family?" His Haitian accent told me that it was Fedore's bitch ass. Then I heard other voices, so I knew they had at least three other men with him. I was outnumbered, but I didn't give a fuck. I didn't hear Dior's voice, and that shook me because she was pregnant with my seed.

"You told her to get inside the nigga's head. What did you expect?" That was another Haitian voice.

"Now we ain't gon' know where that nigga lay his head," Fedore said as I moved closer to where their voices were coming from. I got close to the door and eased it open and noticed that all their backs were to me. Fedore turned to the side, and I noticed him wiping blood off his hands with a towel. My eyes went to the floor, and there laid Dior dead as a fucking doorknob. I don't know if it was the fact that I had feelings for her or that she was pregnant with my baby, but I ambushed them bitches, letting my fucking gun rip until it was out of bullets. They tried to shoot back, but only one bullet grazed my arm. I still let my shit rip until they were no longer shooting.

When the dust settled, all of them were dead. I'd come over here to kill Dior because that was the only way for me and my wife to heal, but I guess they beat me to the punch. I grabbed my phone and dialed my cleanup crew.

"Cleanup in the burbs." I hung the phone up and slipped back in my car, unseen and unheard.

I drove straight to Mahyesha's house because I needed stitches and I wasn't going to the hospital.

"What the fuck happened to you, boy?" Mahyesha swung the door open noticing the blood that soaked through my shirt.

"It's just a flesh wound and I want you to fix it." She opened the door wider to let me in.

"Somebody beat me to her," I told my mother as I sat at the island while she got the first-aid kit.

"It was Fhendi's brother and his goons, but I killed all them bitches because they killed her," I told my mother, and she grabbed my face.

"Did you kill them Haitians because she was pregnant, or because you were mad that they got to her first?" she asked me, and I thought about her question. Although she was pregnant, I was going to kill her.

"I was mad as fuck because they killed her before I got there. I wanted to be the last face she saw before she met her husband in hell." I laughed as she cut my shirt and started to bandage me up.

"Karma is a bitch, ain't it? It ain't got no expiration date," she said, and I was confused.

"Don't look at me like that. Now you know how it feels to kill your own child whether inside or outside of the womb," she said, and I sat back and thought. I killed my unborn child and Chunky killed my daughter. I guess we were somewhat even.

"Son, listen to me, Zenobia didn't mean to kill Mhyia, and there is no real explanation as to why she did it. I told you before, post-partum ain't fuck to play with. Now charter the jet and go get yo' damn family, including MJ." She winked her eye at me, and I smiled. I already knew she told Zenobia, because that's the type of messy shit she did. She didn't bite her tongue about shit, and that's what I loved about my mother the most.

It took two hours between me getting on the jet and making it to Chunky's condo. It was late afternoon, so I knew the kids were asleep. When I heard the rapper Trina's voice, I knew it was gon' be some shit. I knocked on the door, but I doubted if she would hear me. I waited a few minutes, then I started knocking harder. She swung the door open, looking scrumptious. She had on a black t-shirt with boy shorts and white painted toes. She looked up at me with her hands on her hips.

"Oh, now you wanna show yo' fucking face." I pushed her ass in the door and shut it behind me.

I backed her all the way to her counter, wrapping her up in my arms. She tried to play hard and not hug me back, until palmed her ass cheeks and massaged them. She must have forgot I knew that shit turned her on. Her hands grazed the side of my arm from the bullet, and she smirked.

"You got a war wound trying to kill that bitch, huh?" She kissed my bandage before looking at me.

"I was outnumbered," I told her.

"Did you kill all of them?" she asked me, and I nodded my head up and down, and she smiled. I bent down and kissed her lips. She slid her tongue in my mouth, and I sucked on it.

"Where ya lil' friend at?" I asked her, being petty.

"You mean your son?" She cocked her head to the side, and I knew Mahyesha had ran her fucking mouth.

"Don't look fucking stupid. Mahyesha told me because you know she can't hold water on her fucking tongue, but I felt that shit. When I first met MJ after you left me, I knew he was different. Everything about him was different. He didn't want to fuck me or anything, we just vibed and talked. He told about his mother, and I shared some things with him. He reminded me so much of you, and I think that's why I gravitated more to him but in a brotherly way. No, he is not here. I haven't seen him in days because whatever his maw told him made him mad, and when he got here his energy was off. He told me who he was then left, and I haven't seen him since," she said as I caressed her fluffy ass body. I didn't hear shit she was saying because my dick was hard as fuck, and I was ready to put another baby in her thick ass.

"Are you listening to me, Mahsyn?" I hadn't heard her call me that in so long it made my dick harder. I palmed her pussy, and she moaned.

"You killed Candyce?" I asked as I slipped my fingers inside of her and moved them in and out.

"Are you still free?" she moaned and bit her bottom lip, throwing her pussy against my fingers.

"You feel me, right?" I sucked her top lip before she could answer.

"Then I killed that bitch." She smiled, and I knew I created a monster. She opened her legs more to give me better access to her wet-wet.

"This pussy got big for Daddy, huh?" I looked into her lazy eyes.

"It been big for you, Mahsyn." She kissed my neck, and I worked my hands faster.

"The food gon' burn, Mahsyn, we gotta stop," she moaned, still licking my neck. She didn't want me to stop.

"Fuck that food, Chunky. I want this pussy." I lifted her thighs and sat her on the counter. I pulled my dick out my joggers and rubbed it against her opening.

"Just put the head in, Mahsyn, before the kids come in here." Her body trembled. She was feigning for the dick. I loved teasing her. It made the sex more intense when she begged for it.

"Just the head, Chunky? That's all you want?" I rubbed it up and down her clit. I knew she was about to nut. Her head fell back.

I pushed into her inch by inch. She scooted her ass closer to the end of the counter and lifted her ass up to meet me halfway. She rolled her hips against me with her elbows against the tiled counter. All I had to do was stand there, because she was taking the dick. I raised her shirt up and sucked her titties as she rode my dick. I palmed her ass as I met her thrust for thrust, because she wasn't about to fuck me. I was doing the fucking.

"Fuck, Magnolia," she moaned as she rode faster and faster. I couldn't control her pussy as it contracted around my shaft. My nut was rising to the tip of my dick as her nut wet me up.

"The fuck did I just walk in on?" We both froze as I turned around and looked into the eyes of MJ. His hand went to his eyes as he tried to walk past us.

"Y'all motherfuckers nasty, I'ma go check on the kids. Y'all 'bout to burn this motherfucker down and we hungry." He laughed as I pulled Chunky's shirt down and pulled her off the counter. We both busted out laughing as she jumped down and walked over to the pots and continued to cook.

I went to the bathroom to clean myself up, because I needed to have a long overdue conversation with my son. I walked into the living room where MJ held Mhayce and Zheno was on side of him. The twins were engrossed with their tablets. I picked Zheno up and sat down with him laying on my chest.

"I didn't know you existed." I started the conversation to break the ice.

"I know you didn't, but my mother told me everything," he said, and I knew what everything meant.

"Listen, it's not that I didn't want you, we were young and I was in the streets. I know that's not an excuse for wanting Mariah to abort you, but for what it's worth, I'm glad she didn't." I held my hand out, and he dapped me up.

"I can't control the past but moving forward, I wanna know you more and I want you with me. I can't raise you because the streets did that already, but I wanna be a part of your life and help you make better decisions. I want you by my side instead of against me," I told him, and he nodded his head in agreement.

"If you wanna be a kingpin or go to college, I'm fucking with it, but how you was moving wasn't safe. I just want to help you move safer," I told him.

"Believe it or not, Nobby was sparing a nigga. I was wilding until I ran across her," he told me, and I smiled because she had that effect on everybody.

"I can believe it. Now you got siblings and a bonus mom that will love you through the good and bad, but in a week or two, we going back home," I told him.

"And where is that?" he asked me.

"Georgia," I told him, and he smiled.

EPILOGUE

ZENOBIA

ONE YEAR LATER

This was one hell of a fucking ride to get to this point, but if I had to do it all over again, I would. Five books later, a bunch of dead bitches, throw in some cheating and bonus kids, and you have our love story. It ain't perfect but it's ours, and we enjoyed the ride. I can't believe we lasted this long, but y'all kept asking for my husband and y'all had to know I wouldn't be too far behind, because he is mine. I was never going nowhere. I didn't care who he was fucking and who got pregnant. Y'all thought I didn't know about that, but I did. I just didn't give a fuck because I knew Magnolia would handle that shit, and some shit was better left unsaid. I been had a calm spirit, so the shit Magnolia did would never rock me, and I'd done my share of shit too.

Two weeks after Magnolia talked to MJ, we packed up and left New Orleans for good this time, and we took MJ with us. Our family was finally whole and all threats were dead. When Magnolia went to court, of course, the CI didn't show up, so the case was thrown out. I don't know nor do I give a fuck about Dior and her death, because I mind the business that pays me.

I don't know why Miss Jazzie tried to make y'all think that I could be replaced with the next bitch, but she tried it. It kinda worked, but Magnolia not stupid. He know where it's good at. There was never a fucking Magnolia and Dior, she just spelled my fucking name wrong. It will always be Magnolia and Zenobia. Nah let us do us and wait on the next set of dysfunctional people, because we done for real this time.

BBYYYYEEEEEEEEEEEE

ALSO BY MISS. JAZZIE

Made in the USA
Middletown, DE
24 August 2023

37289242R00064